The Captain's Doll

D. H. Lawrence

The Captain's Doll

The present edition is a reproduction of previous publication of this classic work. Minor typographical errors may have been corrected without note, however, for an authentic reading experience the spelling, punctuation, and capitalization have been retained from the original text.

ISBN: 978-1-64439-034-4

Table of Contents

Chapter 1

'Hannele!'

'Ja — a.'

'Wo bist du?'

'Hier.'

'Wo dann?'

Hannele did not lift her head from her work. She sat in a low chair under a reading-lamp, a basket of coloured silk pieces beside her, and in her hands a doll, or mannikin, which she was dressing. She was doing something to the knee of the mannikin, so that the poor little gentleman flourished head downwards with arms wildly tossed out. And it was not at all seemly, because the doll was a Scotch soldier in tight-fitting tartan trews.

There was a tap at the door, and the same voice, a woman's, calling:

'Hannele?'

'Ja — a!'

'Are you here? Are you alone?' asked the voice in German.

'Yes — come in.'

Hannele did not sound very encouraging. She turned round her doll as the door opened, and straightened his coat. A dark-eyed young woman peeped in through the door, with a roguish coyness. She was dressed fashionably for the street, in a thick cape-wrap, and a little black hat pulled down to her ears.

'Quite, quite alone!' said the newcomer, in a tone of wonder. 'Where is he, then?'

'That I don't know,' said Hannele.

'And you sit here alone and wait for him? But no! That I call courage! Aren't you afraid?' Mitchka strolled across to her friend.

'Why shall I be afraid?' said Hannele curtly.

'But no! And what are you doing? Another puppet! He is a good one, though! Ha — ha — ha! HIM! It is him! No — no — that is too beautiful! No — that is too beautiful, Hannele. It is him — exactly him. Only the trousers.'

'He wears those trousers too,' said Hannele, standing her doll on her knee. It was a perfect portrait of an officer of a Scottish regiment, slender, delicately made, with a slight, elegant stoop of the shoulders and close-fitting tartan trousers. The face was beautifully modelled, and a wonderful portrait, dark-skinned, with a little, close-cut, dark moustache, and wide-open dark eyes, and that air of aloofness and perfect diffidence which marks an officer and a gentleman.

Mitchka bent forward, studying the doll. She was a handsome woman with a warm, dark golden skin and clear black eyebrows over her russet-brown eyes.

'No,' she whispered to herself, as if awe-struck. 'That is him. That is him. Only not the trousers. Beautiful, though, the trousers. Has he really such beautiful fine legs?'

Hannele did not answer.

'Exactly him. Just as finished as he is. Just as complete. He is just like that: finished off. Has he seen it?'

'No,' said Hannele.

'What will he say, then?' She started. Her quick ear had caught a sound on the stone stairs. A look of fear came to her face. She flew to the door and out of the room, closing the door to behind her.

'Who is it?' her voice was heard calling anxiously down the stairs.

The answer came in German. Mitchka immediately opened the door again and came back to join Hannele.

'Only Martin,' she said.

She stood waiting. A man appeared in the doorway — erect, military.

'Ah! Countess Hannele,' he said in his quick, precise way, as he stood on the threshold in the distance. 'May one come in?'

'Yes, come in,' said Hannele.

The man entered with a quick, military step, bowed, and kissed the hand of the woman who was sewing the doll. Then, much more intimately, he touched Mitchka's hands with his lips.

Mitchka meanwhile was glancing round the room. It was a very large attic, with the ceiling sloping and then bending in two handsome movements towards the walls. The light from the dark-shaded reading-lamp fell softly on the huge whitewashed vaulting of the ceiling, on the various objects round the walls, and made a brilliant pool of colour where Hannele sat in her soft, red dress, with her basket of silks.

She was a fair woman with dark-blond hair and a beautiful fine skin. Her face seemed luminous, a certain quick gleam of life about it as she looked up at the man. He was handsome, clean-shaven, with very blue eyes strained a little too wide. One could see the war in his face.

Mitchka was wandering round the room, looking at everything, and saying: 'Beautiful! But beautiful! Such good taste! A man, and such good taste! No, they don't need a woman. No, look here, Martin, the Captain Hepburn has arranged all this room himself. Here you have the man. Do you see? So simple, yet so elegant. He needs a woman.'

The room was really beautiful, spacious, pale, soft-lighted. It was heated by a large stove of dark-blue tiles, and had very little furniture save large peasant cupboards or presses of painted wood, and a huge writing-table, on which were writing materials and some scientific apparatus and a cactus plant with fine scarlet blossoms. But it was a man's room. Tobacco and pipes were on a little tray, on the pegs in the distance hung military overcoats and belts, and two guns on a bracket. Then there were two telescopes, one mounted on a stand near a window. Various astronomical apparatus lay upon the table.

'And he reads the stars. Only think — he is an astronomer and reads the stars. Queer, queer people, the English!'

'He is Scottish,' said Hannele.

'Yes, Scottish,' said Mitchka. 'But, you know, I am afraid when I am with him. He is at a closed end. I don't know where I can get to with him. Are you afraid of him too, Hannele? Ach, like a closed road!'

'Why should I be?'

'Ah, you! Perhaps you don't know when you should be afraid. But if he were to come and find us here? No, no — let us go. Let us go, Martin. Come, let us go. I don't want the Captain Hepburn to come and find me in his room. Oh no!' Mitchka was busily pushing Martin to the door, and he was laughing with the queer, mad laugh in his strained eyes. 'Oh no! I don't like. I don't like it,' said Mitchka, trying her English now. She spoke a few sentences prettily. 'Oh no, Sir Captain, I don't want that you come. I don't like it, to be here when you come. Oh no. Not at all. I go. I go, Hannele. I go, my Hannele. And you will really stay here and wait for him? But when will he come? You don't know? Oh dear, I don't like it, I don't like it. I do not wait in the man's room. No, no — Never — jamais — jamais, voyez-vous. Ach, you poor

Hannele! And he has got wife and children in England? Nevair! No, nevair shall I wait for him.'

She had bustlingly pushed Martin through the door and settled her wrap and taken a mincing, elegant pose, ready for the street, and waved her hand and made wide, scared eyes at Hannele, and was gone. The Countess Hannele picked up the doll again and began to sew its shoe. What living she now had she earned making these puppets.

But she was restless. She pressed her arms into her lap, as if holding them bent had wearied her. Then she looked at the little clock on his writing-table. It was long after dinner-time — why hadn't he come? She sighed rather exasperated. She was tired of her doll.

Putting aside her basket of silks, she went to one of the windows. Outside the stars seemed white, and very near. Below was the dark agglomeration of the roofs of houses, a fume of light came up from beneath the darkness of roofs, and a faint breakage of noise from the town far below. The room seemed high, remote, in the sky.

She went to the table and looked at his letter-clip with letters in it, and at his sealing-wax and his stamp-box, touching things and moving them a little, just for the sake of the contrast, not really noticing what she touched. Then she took a pencil, and in stiff Gothic characters began to write her name — Johanna zu Rassentlow — time after time her own name — and then once, bitterly, curiously, with a curious sharpening of her nose: Alexander Hepburn.

But she threw the pencil down, having no more interest in her writing. She wandered to where the large telescope stood near a farther window, and stood for some minutes with her fingers on the barrel, where it was a little brighter from his touching it. Then she drifted restlessly back to her chair. She had picked up her puppet when she heard him on the stairs. She lifted her face and watched as he entered.

'Hello, you there!' he said quietly, as he closed the door behind him. She glanced at him swiftly, but did not move or answer.

He took off his overcoat with quick, quiet movements, and went to hang it up on the pegs. She heard his step, and looked again. He was like the doll, a tall, slender, well-bred man in uniform. When he turned, his dark eyes seemed very wide open. His black hair was growing grey at the temples — the first touch.

She was sewing her doll. Without saying anything, he wheeled round the chair from the writing-table, so that he sat with his knees almost touching her. Then he crossed one leg over the other. He wore fine tartan socks. His ankles seemed slender and elegant, his brown shoes fitted as if they were part of him. For some moments he watched her as she sat sewing. The light fell on her soft, delicate hair, that was full of strands of gold and of tarnished gold and shadow. She did not look up.

In silence he held out his small, naked-looking brown hand for the doll. On his fore-arm were black hairs.

She glanced up at him. Curious how fresh and luminous her face looked in contrast to his.

'Do you want to see it?' she asked, in natural English.

'Yes,' he said.

She broke off her thread of cotton and handed him the puppet. He sat with one leg thrown over the other, holding the doll in one hand and smiling inscrutably with his dark eyes. His hair, parted perfectly on one side, was jet black and glossy.

'You've got me,' he said at last, in his amused, melodious voice.

'What?' she said.

'You've got me,' he repeated.

'I don't care,' she said.

'What — You don't care?' His face broke into a smile. He had an odd way of answering, as if he were only half attending, as if he were thinking of something else.

'You are very late, aren't you?' she ventured.

'Yes. I am rather late.'

'Why are you?'

'Well, as a matter of fact, I was talking with the Colonel.'

'About me?'

'Yes. It was about you.'

She went pale as she sat looking up into his face. But it was impossible to tell whether there was distress on his dark brow or not.

'Anything nasty?' she said.

'Well, yes. It was rather nasty. Not about you, I mean. But rather awkward for me.'

She watched him. But still he said no more.

'What was it?' she said.

'Oh, well — only what I expected. They seem to know rather too much about you — about you and me, I mean. Not that anybody cares one bit, you know, unofficially. The trouble is, they are apparently going to have to take official notice.'

'Why?'

'Oh, well — it appears my wife has been writing letters to the Major-General. He is one of her family acquaintances — known her all his life. And I suppose she's been hearing rumours. In fact, I know she has. She said so in her letter to me.'

'And what do you say to her then?'

'Oh, I tell her I'm all right — not to worry.'

'You don't expect THAT to stop her worrying, do you?' she asked.

'Oh, I don't know. Why should she worry?' he said.

'I think she might have some reason,' said Hannele. 'You've not seen her for a year. And if she adores you — '

'Oh, I don't think she adores me. I think she quite likes me.'

'Do you think you matter as little as that to her?'

'I don't see why not. Of course she likes to feel SAFE about me.'

'But now she doesn't feel safe?'

'No — exactly. Exactly. That's the point. That's where it is. The Colonel advises me to go home on leave.'

He sat gazing with curious, bright, dark, unseeing eyes at the doll which he held by one arm. It was an extraordinary likeness of himself, true even to the smooth parting of his hair and his peculiar way of fixing his dark eyes.

'For how long?' she asked.

'I don't know. For a month,' he replied, first vaguely, then definitely.

'For a month!' She watched him, and seemed to see him fade from her eyes.

'And will you go?' she asked.

'I don't know. I don't know.' His head remained bent, he seemed to muse rather vaguely. 'I don't know,' he repeated. 'I can't make up my mind what I shall do.'

'Would you like to go?' she asked.

He lifted his brows and looked at her. Her heart always melted in her when he looked straight at her with his black eyes and that curious, bright, unseeing look that was more like second sight than direct human vision. She never knew what he saw when he looked at her.

'No,' he said simply. 'I don't WANT to go. I don't think I've any desire at all to go to England.'

'Why not?' she asked.

'I can't say.' Then again he looked at her, and a curious white light seemed to shine on his eyes, as he smiled slowly with his mouth, and said: 'I suppose you ought to know, if anybody does.'

A glad, half-frightened look came on her face.

'You mean you don't want to leave me?' she asked, breathless.

'Yes. I suppose that's what I mean.'

'But you aren't sure?'

'Yes, I am, I'm quite sure,' he said, and the curious smile lingered on his face, and the strange light shone in his eyes.

'That you don't want to leave me?' she stammered, looking aside.

'Yes, I'm quite sure I don't want to leave you,' he repeated. He had a curious, very melodious Scottish voice. But it was the incomprehensible smile on his face that convinced and frightened her. It was almost a gargoyle smile, a strange, lurking, changeless-seeming grin.

She was frightened, and turned aside her face. When she looked at him again, his face was like a mask, with strange, deep-graven lines and a glossy dark skin and a fixed look — as if carved half grotesquely in some glossy stone. His black hair on his smooth, beautifully-shaped head seemed changeless.

'Are you rather tired?' she asked him.

'Yes, I think I am.' He looked at her with black, unseeing eyes and a mask-like face. Then he glanced as if he heard something. Then he rose with his hand on his belt, saying: 'I'll take off my belt and change my coat, if you don't mind.'

He walked across the room, unfastening his broad, brown belt. He was in well-fitting, well-cut khaki. He hung up his belt and came back to her wearing an old, light tunic, which he left unbuttoned. He carried his slippers in one hand. When he sat down to unfasten his shoes, she noticed again how black and hairy his fore-arm was, how naked his brown hand seemed. His hair was black and smooth and perfect on his head, like some close helmet, as he stooped down.

He put on his slippers, carried his shoes aside, and resumed his chair, stretching luxuriously.

'There,' he said. 'I feel better now.' And he looked at her. 'Well,' he said, 'and how are you?'

'Me?' she said. 'Do I matter?' She was rather bitter.

'Do you matter?' he repeated, without noticing her bitterness. 'Why, what a question! Of course you are of the very highest importance. What? Aren't you?' And smiling his curious smile — it made her for a moment think of the fixed sadness of monkeys, of those Chinese carved soapstone apes. He put his hand under her chin, and gently drew his finger along her cheek. She flushed deeply,

'But I'm not as important as you, am I?' she asked defiantly.

'As important as me! Why, bless you, I'm not important a bit. I'm not important a bit!' — the odd straying sound of his words mystified her. What did he really mean?

'And I'm even less important than that,' she said bitterly.

'Oh no, you're not. Oh no, you're not. You're very important. You're very important indeed, I assure you.'

'And your wife?' — the question came rebelliously. 'Your wife? Isn't she important?'

'My wife? My wife?' He seemed to let the word stray out of him as if he did not quite know what it meant. 'Why, yes, I suppose she is important in her own sphere.'

'What sphere?' blurted Hannele, with a laugh.

'Why, her own sphere, of course. Her own house, her own home, and her two children: that's her sphere.'

'And you? — where do you come in?'

'At present I don't come in,' he said.

'But isn't that just the trouble,' said Hannele. 'If you have a wife and a home, it's your business to belong to it, isn't it?'

'Yes, I suppose it is, if I want to,' he replied.

'And you DO want to?' she challenged.

'No, I don't,' he replied.

'Well, then?' she said.

'Yes, quite,' he answered. 'I admit it's a dilemma.'

'But what will you DO?' she insisted.

'Why, I don't know. I don't know yet. I haven't made up my mind what I'm going to do.'

'Then you'd better begin to make it up,' she said.

'Yes, I know that. I know that.'

He rose and began to walk uneasily up and down the room. But the same vacant darkness was on his brow. He had his hands in his pockets. Hannele sat feeling helpless. She couldn't help being in love with the man: with his hands, with his strange, fascinating physique, with his incalculable presence. She loved the way he put his feet down, she loved the way he moved his legs as he walked, she loved the mould of his loins, she loved the way he dropped his head a little, and the strange, dark vacancy of his brow, his not-thinking. But now the restlessness only made her unhappy. Nothing would come of it. Yet she had driven him to it.

He took his hands out of his pockets and returned to her like a piece of iron returning to a magnet. He sat down again in front of her and put his hands out to her, looking into her face.

'Give me your hands,' he said softly, with that strange, mindless, soft, suggestive tone which left her powerless to disobey. 'Give me your hands, and let me feel that we are together. Words mean so little. They mean nothing. And all that one thinks and plans doesn't amount to anything. Let me feel that we are together, and I don't care about all the rest.'

He spoke in his slow, melodious way, and closed her hands in his. She struggled still for voice.

'But you'll HAVE to care about it. You'll HAVE to make up your mind. You'll just HAVE to,' she insisted.

'Yes, I suppose I shall. I suppose I shall. But now that we are together, I won't bother. Now that we are together, let us forget it.'

'But when we CAN'T forget it any more?'

'Well — then I don't know. But — tonight — it seems to me — we might just as well forget it.'

The soft, melodious, straying sound of his voice made her feel helpless. She felt that he never answered her. Words of reply seemed to stray out of him, in the need to say SOMETHING. But he himself never spoke. There he was, a continual blank silence in front of her.

She had a battle with herself. When he put his hand again on her cheek, softly, with the most extraordinary soft half-touch, as a kitten's paw sometimes touches one, like a fluff of living air, then, if it had not been for the magic of that almost indiscernible caress of his hand, she would have stiffened herself and drawn away and told him she could have nothing to do with him, while he was so half-hearted and unsatisfactory. She wanted to tell him these things. But when she began he answered invariably in the same soft, straying voice, that seemed to spin gossamer threads all over her, so that she could neither think nor act nor even feel distinctly. Her soul groaned rebelliously in her. And yet, when he put his hand softly under her chin, and lifted her face and smiled down on her with that gargoyle smile of his — she let him kiss her.

'What are you thinking about tonight?' he said. 'What are you thinking about?'

'What did your Colonel say to you, exactly?' she replied, trying to harden her eyes.

'Oh, that!' he answered. 'Never mind that. That is of no significance whatever.'

'But what IS of any significance?' she insisted. She almost hated him.

'What is of any significance? Well, nothing to me, outside of this room at this minute. Nothing in time or space matters to me.'

'Yes, THIS MINUTE!' she repeated bitterly. 'But then there's the future. I'VE got to live in the future.'

'The future! The future! The future is used up every day. The future to me is like a big tangle of black thread. Every morning you begin to untangle one loose end — and that's your day. And every evening you break off and throw away what you've untangled, and the heap is so much less: just one thread less, one day less. That's all the future matters to me.'

'Then nothing matters to you. And I don't matter to you. As you say, only an end of waste thread,' she resisted him.

'No, there you're wrong. You aren't the future to me.'

'What am I then? — the past?'

'No, not any of those things. You're nothing. As far as all that goes, you're nothing.'

'Thank you,' she said sarcastically, 'if I'm nothing.'

But the very irrelevancy of the man overcame her. He kissed her with half discernible, dim kisses, and touched her throat. And the meaninglessness of him fascinated her and left her powerless. She could ascribe no meaning to him, none whatever. And yet his mouth, so strange in kissing, and his hairy forearms, and his slender, beautiful breast with black hair — it was all like a mystery to her, as if one of the men from Mars were loving her. And she was heavy and spellbound, and she loved the spell that bound her. But also she didn't love it.

Chapter 2

Countess zu Rassentlow had a studio in one of the main streets. She was really a refugee. And nowadays you can be a grand-duke and a pauper, if you are a refugee. But Hannele was not a pauper, because she and her friend Mitchka had the studio where they made these dolls, and beautiful cushions of embroidered coloured wools, and such-like objects of feminine art. The dolls were quite famous, so the two women did not starve.

Hannele did not work much in the studio. She preferred to be alone in her own room, which was another fine attic, not quite so large as the captain's, under the same roof. But often she went to the studio in the afternoon, and if purchasers came, then they were offered a cup of tea.

The Alexander doll was never intended for sale. What made Hannele take it to the studio one afternoon, we do not know. But she did so, and stood it on a little bureau. It was a wonderful little portrait of an officer and gentleman, the physique modelled so that it made you hold your breath.

'And THAT— that is genius!' cried Mitchka. 'That is a chef d'oeuvre! That is thy masterpiece, Hannele. That is really marvellous. And beautiful! A beautiful man, what! But no, that is TOO real. I don't understand how you DARE. I always thought you were GOOD, Hannele, so much better-natured than I am. But now you frighten me. I am afraid you are wicked, do you know. It frightens me to think that you are wicked. Aber nein! But you won't leave him there?'

'Why not?' said Hannele, satiric.

Mitchka made big dark eyes of wonder, reproach, and fear.

'But you MUST not,' she said.

'Why not?'

'No, that you MAY not do. You love the man.'

'What then?'

'You can't leave his puppet standing there.'

'Why can't I?'

'But you are really wicked. Du bist wirklich bös. Only think! — and he is an English officer.'

'He isn't sacrosanct even then.'

'They will expel you from the town. They will deport you.'

'Let them, then.'

'But no! What will you do? That would be horrible if we had to go to Berlin or to Munich and begin again. Here everything has happened so well.'

'I don't care,' said Hannele.

Mitchka looked at her friend and said no more. But she was angry. After some time she turned and uttered her ultimatum.

'When you are not there,' she said, 'I shall put the puppet away in a drawer. I shall show it to nobody, nobody. And I must tell you, it makes me afraid to see it there. It makes me afraid. And you have no right to get me into trouble, do you see. It is not I who look at the English officers. I don't like them, they are too cold and finished off for me. I shall never bring trouble on MYSELF because of the English officers.'

'Don't be afraid,' said Hannele. 'They won't trouble YOU. They know everything we do, well enough. They have their spies everywhere. Nothing will happen to you.'

'But if they make you go away — and I am planted here with the studio — '

It was no good, however; Hannele was obstinate.

So, one sunny afternoon there was a ring at the door: a little lady in white, with a wrinkled face that still had its prettiness.

'Good afternoon!' — in rather lardy-dardy, middle-class English. 'I wonder if I may see your things in your studio.'

'Oh yes!' said Mitchka. 'Please come in.'

Entered the little lady in her finery and her crumpled prettiness. She would not be very old: perhaps younger than fifty. And it was odd that her face had gone so crumpled, because her figure was very trim, her eyes were bright, and she had pretty teeth when she laughed. She was very fine in her clothes: a dress of thick knitted white silk, a large ermine scarf with the tails only at the ends, and a black hat over which dripped a trail of green feathers of the osprey sort. She wore rather a lot of jewellery, and two bangles tinkled over her white kid gloves as she put up her fingers to touch her hair, whilst she stood complacently and looked round.

'You've got a CHARMING studio — CHARMING— perfectly delightful! I couldn't imagine anything more delightful.'

Mitchka gave a slight ironic bow, and said in her odd, plangent English:

'Oh yes. We like it very much also.'

Hannele, who had dodged behind a screen, now came quickly forth.

'Oh, how do you do!' smiled the elderly lady.' I heard there were two of you. Now which is which, if I may be so bold? This' — and she gave a winsome smile and pointed a white kid finger at Mitchka — 'is the —?'

'Annamaria von Prielau-Carolath,' said Mitchka, slightly bowing.

'Oh!' — and the white kid finger jerked away. 'Then this — '

'Johanna zu Rassentlow,' said Hannele, smiling.

'Ah, yes! Countess von Rassentlow! And this is Baroness von — von — but I shall never remember even if you tell me, for I'm awful at names. Anyhow, I shall call one Countess and the other Baroness. That will do, won't it, for poor me! Now I should like awfully to see your things, if I may. I want to buy a little present to take back to England with me. I suppose I shan't have to pay the world in duty on things like these, shall I?'

'Oh no,' said Mitchka. 'No duty. Toys, you know, they — there is — ' Her English stammered to an end, so she turned to Hannele.

'They don't charge duty on toys, and the embroideries they don't notice,' said Hannele.

'Oh, well. Then I'm all right,' said the visitor. 'I hope I can buy something really nice! I see a perfectly lovely jumper over there, perfectly delightful. But a little too gay for me, I'm afraid. I'm not quite so young as I was, alas.' She smiled her winsome little smile, showing her pretty teeth and the old pearls in her ears shook.

'I've heard so much about your dolls. I hear they're perfectly exquisite, quite works of art. May I see some, please?'

'Oh yes,' came Mitchka's invariable answer, this exclamation being the foundation-stone of all her English.

There were never more than three or four dolls in stock. This time there were only two. The famous captain was hidden in his drawer.

'Perfectly beautiful! Perfectly wonderful!' murmured the little lady, in an artistic murmur. 'I think they're perfectly delightful. It's wonderful of you, Countess, to make them. It is you who make them, is it not? Or do you both do them together?'

Hannele explained, and the inspection and the rhapsody went on together. But it was evident that the little lady was a cautious buyer. She went over the things very carefully, and thought more than twice. The dolls attracted her — but she thought them expensive, and hung fire.

'I do wish,' she said wistfully, 'there had been a larger selection of the dolls. I feel, you know, there might have been one which I JUST LOVED. Of course these are DARLINGS— darlings they are: and worth every PENNY, considering the work there is in them. And the art, of course. But I have a feeling, don't you know how it is, that if there had been just one or two more, I should have found one which I ABSOLUTELY couldn't live without. Don't you know how it is? One is so foolish, of course. What does Goethe say — "Dort wo du nicht bist. . ."? My German isn't even a beginning, so you must excuse it. But it means you always feel you would be happy somewhere else, and not just where you are. Isn't that it? Ah, well, it's so very often true — so very often. But not always, thank goodness.' She smiled an odd little smile to herself, pursed her lips, and resumed: 'Well now, that's how I feel about the dolls. If only there had been one or two more. Isn't there a single one?'

She looked winsomely at Hannele.

'Yes,' said Hannele, 'there is one. But it is ordered. It isn't for sale.'

'Oh, do you think I might see it? I'm sure it's lovely. Oh, I'm dying to see it. You know what woman's curiosity is, don't you?' — she laughed her tinkling little laugh. 'Well, I'm afraid I'm all woman, unfortunately. One is so much harder if one has a touch of the man in one, don't you think, and more able to bear things. But I'm afraid I'm all woman.' She sighed and became silent.

Hannele went quietly to the drawer and took out the captain. She handed him to the little woman. The latter looked frightened. Her eyes became round and childish, her face went yellowish. Her jewels tinkled nervously as she stammered:

'Now THAT— isn't that — ' and she laughed a little, hysterical laugh.

She turned round, as if to escape.

'Do you mind if I sit down,' she said. 'I think the standing — ' and she subsided into a chair. She kept her face averted. But she held the puppet fast, her small, white fingers with their heavy jewelled rings clasped round his waist.

'You know,' rushed in Mitchka, who was terrified. 'You know, that is a life picture of one of the Englishmen, of a gentleman, you know. A life picture, you know.'

'A portrait,' said Hannele brightly.

'Yes,' murmured the visitor vaguely. 'I'm sure it is. I'm sure it is a very clever portrait indeed.'

She fumbled with a chain, and put up a small gold lorgnette before her eyes, as if to screen herself. And from behind the screen of her lorgnette she peered at the image in her hand.

'But,' she said, 'none of the English officers, or rather Scottish, wear the close-fitting tartan trews any more — except for fancy dress.'

Her voice was vague and distant.

'No, they don't now,' said Hannele. 'But that is the correct dress. I think they are so handsome, don't you?'

'Well. I don't know. It depends' — and the little woman laughed shakily.

'Oh yes,' said Hannele. 'It needs well-shapen legs.'

'Such as the original of your doll must have had — quite,' said the lady.

'Oh yes,' said Hannele. 'I think his legs are very handsome.'

'Quite!' said the lady. 'Judging from his portrait, as you call it. May I ask the name of the gentleman — if it is not too indiscreet?'

'Captain Hepburn,' said Hannele.

'Yes, of course it is. I knew him at once. I've known him for many years.'

'Oh, please,' broke in Mitchka. 'Oh, please, do not tell him you have seen it! Oh, please! Please do not tell anyone!'

The visitor looked up with a grey little smile.

'But why not?' she said. 'Anyhow, I can't tell him at once, because I hear he is away at present. You don't happen to know when he will be back?'

'I believe tomorrow,' said Hannele.

'Tomorrow!'

'And please!' pleaded Mitchka, who looked lovely in her pleading distress, 'please not to tell anybody that you have seen it.'

'Must I promise?' smiled the little lady wanly. 'Very well, then, I won't tell him I've seen it. And now I think I must be going. Yes, I'll just take the cushion-cover, thank you. Tell me again how much it is, please.'

That evening Hannele was restless. He had been away on some duty for three days. He was returning that night — should have been back in time for dinner. But he had not arrived, and his room was locked and dark. Hannele had heard the servant light the stove some hours ago. Now the room was locked and blank as it had been for three days.

Hannele was most uneasy because she seemed to have forgotten him in the three days whilst he had been away. He seemed to have quite disappeared out of her. She could hardly even remember him. He had become so insignificant to her she was dazed.

Now she wanted to see him again, to know if it was really so. She felt that he was coming. She felt that he was already putting out some influence towards her. But what? And was he real? Why had she made his doll? Why had his doll been so important, if he was nothing? Why had she shown it to that funny little woman this afternoon? Why was she herself such a fool, getting herself into tangles in this place where it was so unpleasant to be entangled? Why was she entangled, after all? It was all so unreal. And particularly HE was unreal: as unreal as a person in a dream, whom one has never heard of in actual life. In actual life, her own German friends were real. Martin was real: German men were real to her. But this other, he was simply not there. He didn't really exist. He was a nullus, in reality. A nullus — and she had somehow got herself complicated with him.

Was it possible? Was it possible she had been so closely entangled with an absolute nothing? Now he was absent she couldn't even IMAGINE him. He had gone out of her imagination, and even when she looked at his doll she saw nothing but a barren puppet. And yet for this dead puppet she had been compromising herself, now, when it was so risky for her to be compromised.

Her own German friends — her own German men — they were men, they were real beings. But this English officer, he was neither fish, flesh, fowl, nor good red herring, as they say. He was just a hypothetical presence. She felt that if he never came back, she would be just as if she had read a rather peculiar but false story, a tour de force which works up one's imagination all falsely.

Nevertheless, she was uneasy. She had a lurking suspicion that there might be something else. So she kept uneasily wandering out to the landing, and listening to hear if he might be coming.

Yes — there was a sound. Yes, there was his slow step on the stairs, and the slow, straying purr of his voice. And instantly she heard his voice she was afraid again. She knew there WAS something there. And instantly she felt the reality of his presence, she felt the unreality of her own German men friends. The moment she heard the peculiar, slow melody of his foreign voice everything seemed to go changed in her, and Martin and Otto and Albrecht, her German friends, seemed to go pale and dim as if one could almost see through them, like unsubstantial things.

This was what she had to reckon with, this recoil from one to the other. When he was present, he seemed so terribly real. When he was absent he was completely vague, and her own men of her own race seemed so absolutely the only reality.

But he was talking. Who was he talking to? She heard the steps echo up the hollows of the stone staircase slowly, as if wearily, and voices slowly, confusedly mingle. The slow, soft trail of his voice — and then the peculiar, quick tones — yes, of a woman. And not one of the maids, because they were speaking English. She listened hard. The quick, and yet slightly hushed, slightly sad-sounding voice of a woman who talks a good deal, as if talking to herself. Hannele's quick ears caught the sound of what she was saying: 'Yes, I thought the Baroness a perfectly beautiful creature, perfectly lovely. But so extraordinarily like a Spaniard. Do you remember, Alec, at Malaga? I always thought they fascinated you then, with their mantillas. Perfectly lovely she would look in a mantilla. Only perhaps she is too open-hearted, too impulsive, poor thing. She lacks the Spanish reserve. Poor thing, I feel sorry for her. For them both, indeed. It must be very hard to have to do these things for a living, after you've been accustomed to be made much of for your own sake, and for your aristocratic title. It's very hard for them, poor things. Baroness, Countess, it sounds just a little ridiculous, when you're buying woollen embroideries from them. But I suppose, poor things, they can't help it. Better drop the titles altogether, I think— '

'Well, they do, if people will let them. Only English and American people find it so much easier to say Baroness or Countess than Fräulein von Prielau-Carolath, or whatever it is.'

'They could say simply Fräulein, as we do to our governesses — or as we used to, when we HAD German governesses,' came the voice of HER.

'Yes, we COULD,' said his voice.

'After all, what is the good, what is the good of titles if you have to sell dolls and woollen embroideries — not so very beautiful, either.'

'Oh, quite! Oh, quite! I think titles are perhaps a mistake, anyhow. But they've always had them,' came his slow, musical voice, with its sing-song note of hopeless indifference. He sounded rather like a man talking out of his sleep.

Hannele caught sight of the tail of blue-green crane feathers veering round a turn in the stairs away below, and she beat a hasty retreat.

Chapter 3

There was a little platform out on the roof, where he used sometimes to stand his telescope and observe the stars or the moon: the moon when possible. It was not a very safe platform, just a little ledge of the roof, outside the window at the end of the top corridor: or rather, the top landing, for it was only the space between the attics. Hannele had the one attic room at the back, he had the room we have seen, and a little bedroom which was really only a lumber room. Before he came, Hannele had been alone under the roof. His rooms were then lumber room and laundry room, where the clothes were dried. But he had wanted to be high up, because of his stars, and this was the place that pleased him.

Hannele heard him quite late in the night, wandering about. She heard him also on the ledge outside. She could not sleep. He disturbed her. The moon was risen, large and bright in the sky. She heard the bells from the cathedral slowly strike two: two great drops of sound in the livid night. And again, from outside on the roof, she heard him clear his throat. Then a cat howled.

She rose, wrapped herself in a dark wrap, and went down the landing to the window at the end. The sky outside was full of moonlight. He was squatted like a great cat peering up his telescope, sitting on a stool, his knees wide apart. Quite motionless he sat in that attitude, like some leaden figure on the roof. The moonlight glistened with a gleam of plumbago on the great slope of black tiles. She stood still in the window, watching. And he remained fixed and motionless at the end of the telescope.

She tapped softly on the window-pane. He looked round, like some tom-cat staring round with wide night eyes. Then he reached down his hand and pulled the window open.

'Hello,' he said quietly. 'You not asleep?'

'Aren't YOU tired?' she replied, rather resentful.

'No, I was as wide awake as I could be. ISN'T the moon fine tonight! What? Perfectly amazing. Wouldn't you like to come up and have a look at her?'

'No, thank you,' she said hastily, terrified at the thought.

He resumed his posture, peering up the telescope.

'Perfectly amazing,' he said, murmuring. She waited for some time, bewitched likewise by the great October moon and the sky full of resplendent white-green light. It seemed like another sort of day-time. And there he straddled on the roof like some cat! It was exactly like day in some other planet.

At length he turned round to her. His face glistened faintly, and his eyes were dilated like a cat's at night.

'You know I had a visitor?' he said.

'Yes.'

'My wife.'

'Your WIFE!' — she looked up really astonished. She had thought it might be an acquaintance — perhaps his aunt — or even an elder sister. 'But she's years older than you,' she added.

'Eight years,' he said. 'I'm forty-one.'

There was a silence.

'Yes,' he mused. 'She arrived suddenly, by surprise, yesterday, and found me away. She's staying in the hotel, in the Vier Jahreszeiten.'

There was a pause.

'Aren't you going to stay with her?' asked Hannele.

'Yes, I shall probably join her tomorrow.'

There was a still longer pause.

'Why not tonight?' asked Hannele.

'Oh, well — I put it off for tonight. It meant all the bother of my wife changing her room at the hotel — and it was late — and I was all mucky after travelling.'

'But you'll go tomorrow?'

'Yes, I shall go tomorrow. For a week or so. After that I'm not sure what will happen.'

There was quite a long pause. He remained seated on his stool on the roof, looking with dilated, blank, black eyes at nothingness. She stood below in the open window space, pondering.

'Do you want to go to her at the hotel?' asked Hannele.

'Well, I don't, particularly. But I don't mind, really. We're very good friends. Why, we've been friends for eighteen years — we've been married seventeen. Oh, she's a nice little woman. I don't want to hurt her feelings. I wish her no harm, you know. On the contrary, I wish her all the good in the world.'

He had no idea of the blank amazement in which Hannele listened to these stray remarks.

'But — ' she stammered. 'But doesn't she expect you to make LOVE to her?'

'Oh yes, she expects that. You bet she does: woman-like.'

'And you?' — the question had a dangerous ring.

'Why, I don't mind, really, you know, if it's only for a short time.

I'm used to her. I've always been fond of her, you know — and so if it gives her any pleasure — why, I like her to get what pleasure out of life she can.'

'But you — you YOURSELF! Don't YOU feel anything?' Hannele's amazement was reaching the point of incredulity. She began to feel that he was making it up. It was all so different from her own point of view. To sit there so quiet and to make such statements in all good faith: no, it was impossible.

'I don't consider I count,' he said naïvely.

Hannele looked aside. If that wasn't lying, it was imbecility, or worse. She had for the moment nothing to say. She felt he was a sort of psychic phenomenon like a grasshopper or a tadpole or an ammonite. Not to be regarded from a human point of view. No, he just wasn't normal. And she had been fascinated by him! It was only sheer, amazed curiosity that carried her on to her next question.

'But do you NEVER count, then?' she asked, and there was a touch of derision, of laughter in her tone. He took no offence.

'Well — very rarely,' he said. 'I count very rarely. That's how life appears to me. One matters so VERY little.'

She felt quite dizzy with astonishment. And he called himself a man!

'But if you matter so very little, what do you do anything at all for?' she asked.

'Oh, one has to. And then, why not? Why not do things, even if oneself hardly matters. Look at the moon. It doesn't matter in the least to the moon whether I exist or whether I don't. So why should it matter to me?'

After a blank pause of incredulity she said:

'I could die with laughter. It seems to me all so ridiculous — no, I can't believe it.'

'Perhaps it is a point of view,' he said.

There was a long and pregnant silence: we should not like to say pregnant with what.

'And so I don't mean anything to you at all?' she said.

'I didn't say that,' he replied.

'Nothing means anything to you,' she challenged.

'I don't say that.'

'Whether it's your wife — or me — or the moon — toute la même chose.'

'No — no — that's hardly the way to look at it.'

She gazed at him in such utter amazement that she felt something would really explode in her if she heard another word. Was this a man? — or what was it? It was too much for her, that was all.

'Well, good-bye,' she said. 'I hope you will have a nice time at the Vier Jahreszeiten.'

So she left him still sitting on the roof.

'I suppose,' she said to herself, 'that is love à l'anglaise. But it's more than I can swallow.'

Chapter 4

'Won't you come and have tea with me — do! Come right along now. Don't you find it bitterly cold? Yes — well now — come in with me and we'll have a cup of nice, hot tea in our little sitting-room. The weather changes so suddenly, and really one needs a little reinforcement. But perhaps you don't take tea?'

'Oh yes. I got so used to it in England,' said Hannele.

'Did you now! Well now, were you long in England?'

'Oh yes — '

The two women had met in the Domplatz. Mrs Hepburn was looking extraordinarily like one of Hannele's dolls, in a funny little cape of odd striped skins, and a little dark-green skirt, and a rather fuzzy sort of hat. Hannele looked almost huge beside her.

'But now you will come in and have tea, won't you? Oh, please do. Never mind whether it's de rigueur or not. I ALWAYS please myself WHAT I do. I'm afraid my husband gets some shocks sometimes — but that we can't help. I won't have anybody laying down the law to me.' She laughed her winsome little laugh.' So now come along in, and we'll see if there aren't hot scones as well. I love a hot scone for tea in cold weather. And I hope you do. That is, if there are any. We don't know yet.' She tinkled her little laugh. 'My husband may or may not be in. But that makes no difference to you and me, does it? There, it's just striking half past four. In England, we always have tea at half past. My husband ADORES his tea. I don't suppose our man is five minutes off the half past, ringing the gong for tea, not once in twelve months. My husband doesn't mind at all if dinner is a little late. But he gets — quite — well, quite "ratty" if tea is late.' She tinkled a laugh. 'Though I shouldn't say that. He is the soul of kindness and patience. I don't think I've ever known him do an unkind thing — or hardly say an unkind word. But I doubt if he will be in today.'

He WAS in, however, standing with his feet apart and his hands in his trouser pockets in the little sitting-room upstairs in the hotel. He raised his eyebrows the smallest degree, seeing Hannele enter.

'Ah, Countess Hannele — my wife has brought you along! Very nice, very nice! Let me take your wrap. Oh yes, certainly . . .'

'Have you rung for tea, dear?' asked Mrs Hepburn.

'Er — yes. I said as soon as you came in they were to bring it.'

'Yes — well. Won't you ring again, dear, and say for THREE.'

'Yes — certainly. Certainly.'

He rang, and stood about with his hands in his pockets waiting for tea.

'Well now,' said Mrs Hepburn, as she lifted the tea-pot, and her bangles tinkled, and her huge rings of brilliants twinkled, and her big ear-rings of clustered seed-pearls bobbed against her rather withered cheek,' isn't it charming of Countess zu — Countess zu — '

'Rassentlow,' said he. 'I believe most people say Countess Hannele. I know we always do among ourselves. We say Countess Hannele's shop.'

'Countess Hannele's shop! Now, isn't that perfectly delightful: such a romance in the very sound of it. You take cream?'

'Thank you,' said Hannele.

The tea passed in a cloud of chatter, while Mrs Hepburn manipulated the tea-pot, and lit the spirit-flame, and blew it out, and peeped into the steam of the tea-pot, and couldn't see whether there was any more tea or not — and — 'At home I KNOW— I was going to say to a teaspoonful — how much tea there is in the pot. But this tea-pot — I don't know what it's made of — it isn't silver, I know that — it is so heavy in itself that it's deceived me several times already. And my husband is a greedy man, a greedy man — he likes at least three cups — and four if he can get them, or five! Yes, dear, I've plenty of tea today. You shall have even five, if you don't mind the last two weak. Do let me fill your cup, Countess Hannele. I think it's a CHARMING name.'

'There's a play called Hannele, isn't there?' said he.

When he had had his five cups, and his wife had got her cigarette perched in the end of a long, long, slim, white holder, and was puffing like a little Chinawoman from the distance, there was a little lull.

'Alec, dear,' said Mrs Hepburn. 'You won't forget to leave that message for me at Mrs Rackham's. I'm so afraid it will be forgotten.'

'No, dear, I won't forget. Er — would you like me to go round now?'

Hannele noticed how often he said 'er' when he was beginning to speak to his wife. But they WERE such good friends, the two of them.

'Why, if you WOULD, dear, I should feel perfectly comfortable. But I don't want you to hurry one bit.'

'Oh, I may as well go now.'

And he went. Mrs Hepburn detained her guest.

'He IS so charming to me,' said the little woman. 'He's really wonderful. And he always has been the same — invariably. So that if he DID make a little slip — well, you know, I don't have to take it so seriously.'

'No,' said Hannele, feeling as if her ears were stretching with astonishment.

'It's the war. It's just the war. It's had a terribly deteriorating effect on the men.'

'In what way?' said Hannele.

'Why, morally. Really, there's hardly one man left the same as he was before the war. Terribly degenerated.'

'Is that so?' said Hannele.

'It is indeed. Why, isn't it the same with the German men and officers?'

'Yes, I think so,' said Hannele.

'And I'm sure so, from what I hear. But of course it is the women who are to blame in the first place. We poor women! We are a guilty race, I am afraid. But I never throw stones. I know what it is myself to have temptations. I have to flirt a little — and when I was younger — well, the men didn't escape me, I assure you. And I was SO often scorched. But never QUITE singed. My husband never minded. He knew I was REALLY safe. Oh yes, I have always been faithful to him. But still — I have been very near the flame.' And she laughed her winsome little laugh.

Hannele put her fingers to her ears to make sure they were not falling off.

'Of course during the war it was terrible. I know that in a certain hospital it was quite impossible for a girl to stay on if she kept straight. The matrons and sisters just turned her out. They wouldn't have her unless she was one of themselves. And you know what that means. Quite like the convent in Balzac's story — you know which I mean, I'm sure.' And the laugh tinkled gaily.

'But then, what can you expect, when there aren't enough men to go round! Why, I had a friend in Ireland. She and her husband had been an ideal couple, an IDEAL couple. Real playmates. And you can't say more than that, can you? Well, then, he became a major during the war. And she was so looking forward, poor thing, to the perfectly lovely times they would have together when he came home. She is like me, and is lucky enough to have a little income of her own — not a great fortune — but — well — Well now, what was I going to say? Oh yes, she was looking forward to the perfectly lovely times they would have when he came home: building on her dreams, poor thing, as we unfortunate women always do. I suppose we shall never be cured of it.' A little tinkling laugh. 'Well now, not a bit of it. Not a bit of it.' Mrs Hepburn lifted her heavily-jewelled little hand in a motion of protest. It was curious, her hands were pretty and white, and her neck and breast, now she wore a little tea-gown, were also smooth and white and pretty, under the medley of twinkling little chains and coloured jewels. Why should her face have played her this nasty trick of going all crumpled! However, it was so.

'Not one bit of it,' reiterated the little lady. 'He came home quite changed. She said she could hardly recognize him for the same man. Let me tell you one little incident. Just a trifle, but significant. He was coming home — this was some time after he was free from the army — he was coming home from London, and he told her to meet him at the boat: gave her the time and everything. Well, she went to the boat, poor thing, and he didn't come. She waited, and no word of explanation or anything. So she couldn't make up her mind whether to go next day and meet the boat again. However, she decided she wouldn't. So of course, on that boat he arrived. When he got home, he said to her: "Why didn't you meet the boat?" "Well," she said, "I went yesterday, and you didn't come." "Then why didn't you meet it again today?" Imagine it, the sauce! And they had been real playmates. Heart-breaking isn't it? "Well," she said in self-defence, "why didn't you come yesterday?" "Oh," he said, "I met a woman in town whom I liked, and she asked me to spend the night with her, so I did." Now what do you think of that? Can you conceive of such a thing?'

'Oh no,' said Hannele. 'I call that unnecessary brutality.'

'Exactly! So terrible to say such a thing to her! The brutality of it! Well, that's how the world is today. I'm thankful my husband isn't that sort. I don't say he's perfect. But whatever else he did, he'd never be unkind, and he COULDN'T be brutal. He just couldn't. He'd never tell me a lie — I know THAT. But callous brutality, no, thank goodness, he hasn't a spark of it in him. I'm the wicked one, if either of us is wicked.' The little laugh tinkled. 'Oh, but he's been perfect to me, perfect. Hardly a cross word. Why, on our wedding night, he kneeled down in front of me and promised, with God's help, to make my life happy. And I must say, as far as possible, he's kept his word. It has been his one aim in life, to make my life happy.'

The little lady looked away with a bright, musing look towards the window. She was being a heroine in a romance. Hannele could see her being a heroine, playing the chief part in her own life romance. It is such a feminine occupation, that no woman takes offence when she is made audience.

'I'm afraid I've more of the woman than the mother in my composition,' resumed the little heroine. 'I adore my two children. The boy is at Winchester, and my little girl is in a convent in Brittany. Oh, they are perfect darlings, both of them. But the man is first in my mind, I'm afraid. I fear I'm rather old-fashioned. But never mind. I can see the attractions in other men — can't I indeed! There was a perfectly exquisite creature — he was a very clever engineer — but much, much more than THAT. But never mind.' The little heroine sniffed as if there were perfume in the air, folded her jewelled hands, and resumed: 'However — I know what it is myself to flutter round the flame. You know I'm Irish myself, and we Irish can't help it. Oh, I wouldn't be English for anything. Just that little touch of imagination, you know . . .' The little laugh tinkled. 'And that's what makes me able to sympathize with my husband even when, perhaps, I shouldn't. Why, when he was at home with me, he never gave a thought, not a thought to another woman. I must say, he used to make ME feel a little guilty sometimes. But there! I don't think he ever thought of another woman as being flesh and blood, after he knew me. I could tell. Pleasant, courteous, charming — but other women were not flesh and blood to him, they were just people, callers — that kind of thing. It used to amaze me, when some perfectly lovely creature came, whom I should have been head over heels in love with in a minute — and he, he was charming, delightful; he could see her points, but she was no more to him than, let me say, a pot of carnations or a beautiful old piece of punto di Milano. Not flesh and blood. Well, perhaps one can feel too safe. Perhaps one needs a tiny pinch of salt of jealousy. I believe one does. And I have not had one jealous moment for seventeen years. So that, REALLY, when I heard a whisper of something going on here, I felt almost pleased. I felt exonerated for my own little peccadilloes, for one thing. And I felt he was perhaps a little more human. Because, after all, it is nothing but human to fall in love, if you are alone for a long time and in the company of a beautiful woman — and if you're an attractive man yourself.'

Hannele sat with her eyes propped open and her ears buttoned back with amazement, expecting the next revelations.

'Why, of course,' she said, knowing she was expected to say something.

'Yes, of course,' said Mrs Hepburn, eyeing her sharply. 'So I thought I'd better come and see how far things had gone. I had nothing but a hint to go on. I knew no name — nothing. I had just a hint that she was German, and a refugee aristocrat — and that he used to call at the studio.' The little lady eyed Hannele sharply, and gave a breathless little laugh, clasping her hands nervously. Hannele sat absolutely blank: really dazed.

'Of course,' resumed Mrs Hepburn, 'that was enough. That was quite a sufficient clue. I'm afraid my intentions when I called at the studio were not as pure as they might have been. I'm afraid I wanted to see something more than the dolls. But when you showed me HIS doll, then I knew. Of course there wasn't a shadow of doubt after that. And I saw at once that she loved him, poor thing. She was SO agitated. And no idea who I was. And you were so unkind to show me the doll. Of course, you had no idea who you were showing it to. But for her, poor thing, it was such a trial. I could see how she suffered. And I must say she's very lovely — she's very, very lovely, with her golden skin and her reddish amber eyes and her beautiful, beautiful carriage. And such a naïve, impulsive nature. Give everything away in a minute. And then her deep voice — "Oh yes — Oh, please!" — such a child. And such an aristocrat, that lovely turn of her head, and her simple, elegant dress. Oh, she's very charming. And she's just the type I always knew would attract him, if he hadn't got me. I've thought about it many a time — many a time. When a woman is older than a man, she does think these things — especially if he has his attractive points too. And when I've dreamed of the woman he would love if he hadn't got me, it has always been a Spanish type. And the Baroness is extraordinarily Spanish in her appearance. She must have had some noble Spanish ancestor. Don't you think so?'

'Oh yes,' said Hannele.' There were such a lot of Spaniards in Austria, too, with the various emperors.'

'With Charles V, exactly. Exactly. That's how it must have been. And so she has all the Spanish beauty, and all the German feeling. Of course, for myself, I miss the RESERVE, the haughtiness. But she's very, very lovely, and I'm sure I could never HATE her. I couldn't even if I tried. And I'm not going to try. But I think she's much too dangerous for my husband to see much of her. Don't you agree, now?'

'Oh, but really,' stammered Hannele. 'There's nothing in it, really.'

'Well,' said the little lady, cocking her head shrewdly aside, 'I shouldn't like there to be any MORE in it.'

And there was a moment's dead pause. Each woman was reflecting. Hannele wondered if the little lady was just fooling her.

'Anyhow,' continued Mrs Hepburn, 'the spark is there, and I don't intend the fire to spread. I am going to be very, very careful, myself, not to fan the flames. The last thing I should think of would be to make my husband scenes. I believe it would be fatal.'

'Yes,' said Hannele, during the pause.

'I am going very carefully. You think there isn't much in it — between him and the Baroness?'

'No — no — I'm sure there isn't,' cried Hannele, with a full voice of conviction. She was almost indignant at being slighted so completely herself, in the little lady's suspicions.

'Hm! — mm!' hummed the little woman, sapiently nodding her head slowly up and down. 'I'm not so sure! I'm not so sure that it hasn't gone pretty far.'

'Oh NO!' cried Hannele, in real irritation of protest.

'Well,' said the other. 'In any case, I don't intend it to go any farther.'

There was dead silence for some time.

'There's more in it than you say. There's more in it than you say,' ruminated the little woman. 'I know HIM, for one thing. I know he's got a cloud on his brow. And I know it hasn't left his brow for a single minute. And when I told him I had been to the studio, and showed him the cushion-cover, I knew he felt guilty. I am not so easily deceived. We Irish all have a touch of second sight, I believe. Of course I haven't challenged him. I haven't even mentioned the doll. By the way, WHO ordered the doll? Do you mind telling me?'

'No, it wasn't ordered,' confessed Hannele.

'Ah — I thought not — I thought not!' said Mrs Hepburn, lifting her finger. 'At least, I knew no outsider had ordered it. Of course I knew.' And she smiled to herself.

'So,' she continued, 'I had too much sense to say anything about it. I don't believe in stripping wounds bare. I believe in gently covering them and letting them heal. But I DID say I thought her a lovely creature.' The little lady looked brightly at Hannele.

'Yes,' said Hannele.

'And he was very vague in his manner, "Yes, not bad," he said. I thought to myself: Aha, my boy, you don't deceive me with your NOT BAD. She's very much more than not bad. I said so, too. I wanted, of course, to let him know I had a suspicion.'

'And do you think he knew?'

'Of course he did. Of course he did. "She's much too dangerous," I said, "to be in a town where there are so many strange men: married and unmarried." And then he turned round to me and gave himself away, oh, so plainly. "Why?" he said. But such a haughty, distant tone. I said to myself: "It's time, my dear boy, you were removed out of the danger zone." But I answered him: Surely somebody is bound to fall in love with her. Not at all, he said, she keeps to her own countrymen. You don't tell ME, I answered him, with her pretty broken English! It is a wonder the two of them are allowed to stay in the town. And then again he rounded on me. Good gracious! he said. Would you have them turned out just because they're beautiful to look at, when they have nowhere else to go, and they make their bit of a livelihood here? I assure you, he hasn't rounded on me in that overbearing way, not once before, in all our married life. So I just said quietly: I should like to protect OUR OWN MEN. And he didn't say anything more. But he looked at me under his brows and went out of the room.'

There was a silence. Hannele waited with her hands in her lap, and Mrs Hepburn mused, with her hands in HER lap. Her face looked yellow, and VERY wrinkled.

'Well now,' she said, breaking again suddenly into life. 'What are we to do? I mean what is to be done? You are the Baroness's nearest friend. And I wish her NO harm, none whatever.'

'What can we do?' said Hannele, in the pause.

'I have been urging my husband for some time to get his discharge from the army,' said the little woman. 'I knew he could have it in three months' time. But like so many more men, he has no income of his own, and he doesn't want to feel dependent. Perfect nonsense! So he says he wants to stay on in the army. I have never known him before go against my real wishes.'

'But it IS better for a man to be independent,' said Hannele.

'I know it is. But it is also better for him to be AT HOME. And I could get him a post in one of the observatories. He could do something in meteorological work.'

Hannele refused to answer any more.

'Of course,' said Mrs Hepburn, 'if he DOES stay on here, it would be much better if the Baroness left the town.'

'I'm sure she will never leave of her own choice,' said Hannele.

'I'm sure she won't either. But she might be made to see that it would be very much WISER of her to move of her own free will.'

'Why?' said Hannele.

'Why, because she might any time be removed by the British authorities.'

'Why should she?' said Hannele.

'I think the women who are a menace to our men should be removed.'

'But she is NOT a menace to your men.'

'Well, I have my own opinion on that point.'

Which was a decided deadlock.

'I'm sure I've kept you an awful long time with my chatter,' said Mrs Hepburn. 'But I did want to make everything as simple as possible. As I said before, I can't feel any ill-will against her. Yet I can't let things just go on. Heaven alone knows when they may end. Of course if I can persuade my husband to resign his commission and come back to England — anyhow, we will see. I'm sure I am the last person in the world to bear malice.'

The tone in which she said it conveyed a dire threat.

Hannele rose from her chair.

'Oh, and one other thing,' said her hostess, taking out a tiny lace handkerchief and touching her nose delicately with it. 'Do you think' — dab, dab — 'that I might have that DOLL— you know —?'

'That —?'

'Yes, of my husband' — the little lady rubbed her nose with her kerchief.

'The price is three guineas,' said Hannele.

'Oh indeed!' — the tone was very cold. 'I thought it was not for sale.'

Hannele put on her wrap.

'You'll send it round — will you? — if you will be so kind.'

'I must ask my friend first.'

'Yes, of course. But I'm sure she will be so kind as to send it me. It is a little — er — indelicate, don't you think!'

'No,' said Hannele. 'No more than a painted portrait.'

'Don't you?' said her hostess coldly. 'Well, even a painted portrait I think I should like in my own possession. This DOLL— '

Hannele waited, but there was no conclusion.

'Anyhow,' she said, 'the price is three guineas: or the equivalent in marks.'

'Very well,' said the little lady, 'you shall have your three guineas when I get the doll.'

Chapter 5

Hannele went her way pondering. A man never is quite such an abject specimen as his wife makes him look, talking about 'my husband'. Therefore, if any woman wishes to rescue her husband from the clutches of another female, let her only invite this female to tea and talk quite sincerely about 'my husband, you know'. Every man has made a ghastly fool of himself with a woman at some time or other. No woman ever forgets. And most women will give the show away, with real pathos, to another woman. For instance, the picture of Alec at his wife's feet on his wedding night, vowing to devote himself to her life-long happiness — this picture strayed across Hannele's mind time after time, whenever she thought of her dear captain. With disastrous consequences to the captain. Of course if he had been at her own feet, then Hannele would have thought it almost natural: almost a necessary part of the show of love. But at the feet of that other little woman! And what was that other little woman wearing? Her wedding night! Hannele hoped before heaven it wasn't some awful little nightie of frail flowered silk. Imagine it, that little lady! Perhaps in a chic little boudoir cap of punto di Milano, and this slip of frail flowered silk: and the man, perhaps, in his braces! Oh, merciful heaven, save us from other people's indiscretions. No, let us be sure it was in proper evening dress — twenty years ago — very low cut, with a full skirt gathered behind and trailing a little, and a little leather erection in her high-dressed hair, and all those jewels: pearls of course: and he in a dinner-jacket and a white waistcoat: probably in an hotel bedroom in Lugano or Biarritz. And she? Was she standing with one small hand on his shoulder? — or was she seated on the couch in the bedroom? Oh, dreadful thought! And yet it was almost inevitable, that scene. Hannele had never been married, but she had come quite near enough to the realization of the event to know that such a scene WAS practically inevitable. An indispensable part of any honeymoon. Him on his knees, with his heels up!

And how black and tidy his hair must have been then! and no grey at the temples at all. Such a good-looking bridegroom. Perhaps with a white rose in his button-hole still. And she could see him kneeling there, in his new black trousers and a wing collar. And she could see his head bowed. And she could hear his plangent, musical voice saying: 'With God's help, I will make your life happy. I will live for that and for nothing else.' And then the little lady must have had tears in her eyes, and she must have said, rather superbly: 'Thank you, dear, I'm perfectly sure of it.'

Ach! Ach! Husbands should be left to their own wives: and wives should be left to their own husbands. And NO stranger should ever be made a party to these terrible bits of connubial staging. Nay, thought Hannele, that scene was really true. It actually took place. And with the man of that scene I have been in love! With the devoted husband of that little lady. Oh God, oh God, how was it possible! Him on his knees, on his knees, with his heels up!

Am I a perfect fool? she thought to herself. Am I really just an idiot, gaping with love for him? How COULD I? How could I? The very way he says: 'Yes, dear!' to her! The way he does what she tells him! The way he fidgets about the room with his hands in his pockets! The way he goes off when she sends him away because she wants to talk to me. And he knows she wants to talk to me. And he knows what she MIGHT have to say to me. Yet he goes off on his errand without a question, like a servant. 'I will do whatever you wish, darling.' He must have said those words time after time to the little lady. And fulfilled them, also. Performed all his pledges and his promises.

Ach! Ach! Hannele wrung her hands to think of HERSELF being mixed up with him. And he had seemed to her so manly. He seemed to have so much silent male passion in him. And yet — the little lady! 'My husband has ALWAYS been PERFECTLY SWEET to me.' Think of it! On his knees too. And his 'Yes, dear! Certainly. Certainly.' Not that he was afraid of the little lady. He was just committed to her, as he might have been committed to gaol, or committed to paradise.

Had she been dreaming, to be in love with him? Oh, she wished so much she had never been. She WISHED she had never given herself away. To him! — given herself away to him! — and so abjectly. Hung upon his words and his motions, and looked up to him as if he were Caesar. So he had seemed to her: like a mute Caesar. Like Germanicus. Like — she did not know what.

How had it all happened? What had taken her in? Was it just his good looks? No, not really. Because they were the kind of staring good looks she didn't really care for. He must have had charm. He must have charm. Yes, he HAD charm. When it worked.

His charm had not worked on her now for some time — never since that evening after his wife's arrival. Since then he had seemed to her — rather awful. Rather awful — stupid — an ass — a limited, rather vulgar person. That was what he seemed to her when his charm wouldn't work. A limited, rather inferior person. And in a world of Schiebers and profiteers and vulgar, pretentious persons, this was the worst thing possible. A limited, inferior, slightly pretentious individual! The husband of the little lady! And oh heaven, she was so deeply implicated with him! He had not, however, spoken with her in private since his wife's arrival. Probably he would never speak with her in private again. She hoped to heaven, never again. The awful thing was the past, that which had been between him and her. She shuddered when she thought of it. The husband of the little lady!

But surely there was something to account for it! Charm, just charm. He had a charm. And then, oh, heaven, when the charm left off working! It had left off so completely at this moment, in Hannele's case, that her very mouth tasted salt. What DID it all amount to?

What was his charm, after all? How could it have affected her? She began to think of him again, at his best: his presence, when they were alone high up in that big, lonely attic near the stars. His room! — the big white-washed walls, the first scent of tobacco, the silence, the sense of the stars being near, the telescopes, the cactus with fine scarlet flowers: and above all, the strange, remote, insidious silence of his presence, that was so congenial to her also. The curious way he had of turning his head to listen — to listen to what? — as if he heard something in the stars. The strange look, like destiny, in his wide-open, almost staring black eyes. The beautiful lines of his brow, that seemed always to have a certain cloud on it. The slow elegance of his straight, beautiful legs as he walked, and the exquisiteness of his dark, slender chest! Ah, she could feel the charm mounting over her again. She could feel the snake biting her heart. She could feel the arrows of desire rankling.

But then — and she turned from her thoughts back to this last little tea-party in the Vier Jahreszeiten. She thought of his voice: 'Yes, dear. Certainly. Certainly I will.' And she thought of the stupid, inferior look on his face. And the something of a servant-like way in which he went out to do his wife's bidding.

And then the charm was gone again, as the glow of sunset goes off a burning city and leaves it a sordid industrial hole. So much for charm!

So much for charm. She had better have stuck to her own sort of men. Martin, for instance, who was a gentleman and a daring soldier, and a queer soul and pleasant to talk to. Only he hadn't any MAGIC. Magic? The very word made her writhe. Magic? Swindle. Swindle, that was all it amounted to. Magic!

And yet — let us not be too hasty. If the magic had REALLY been there, on those evenings in that great lofty attic. Had it? Yes. Yes, she was bound to admit it. There had been magic. If there had been magic in his presence and in his contact, the husband of the little lady — But the distaste was in her mouth again.

So she started afresh, trying to keep a tight hold on the tail of that all-too-evanescent magic of his. Dear, it slipped so quickly into disillusion. Nevertheless. If it had existed it did exist. And if it did exist, it was worth having. You could call it an illusion if you liked. But an illusion which is a real experience is worth having. Perhaps this disillusion was a greater illusion than the illusion itself. Perhaps all this disillusion of the little lady and the husband of the little lady was falser than the illusion and magic of those few evenings. Perhaps the long disillusion of life was falser than the brief moments of real illusion. After all — the delicate darkness of his breast, the mystery that seemed to come with him as he trod slowly across the floor of his room, after changing his tunic — Nay, nay, if she could keep the illusion of his charm, she would give all disillusion to the devils. Nay, only let her be under the spell of his charm. Only let the spell be upon her. It was all she yearned for. And the thing she had to fight was the vulgarity of disillusion. The vulgarity of the little lady, the vulgarity of the husband of the little lady, the vulgarity of his insincerity, his 'Yes, dear. Certainly! Certainly!' — this was what she had to fight. He WAS vulgar and horrible, then. But also, the queer figure that sat alone on the roof watching the stars! The wonderful red flower of the cactus. The mystery that advanced with him as he came across the room after changing his tunic. The glamour and sadness of him, his silence, as he stooped unfastening his boots. And the strange gargoyle smile, fixed, when he caressed her with his hand under the chin! Life is all a choice. And if she chose the glamour, the magic, the charm, the illusion, the spell! Better death than that other, the husband of the little lady. When all was said and done, was he as much the husband of the little lady as he was that queer, delicate-breasted Caesar of her own knowledge? Which was he?

No, she was NOT going to send her the doll. The little lady should never have the doll.

What a doll she would make herself! Heavens, what a wizened jewel!

Chapter 6

Captain Hepburn still called occasionally at the house for his post. The maid always put his letters in a certain place in the hall, so that he should not have to climb the stairs.

Among his letters — that is to say, along with another letter, for his correspondence was very meagre — he one day found an envelope with a crest. Inside this envelope two letters.

Dear Captain Hepburn,

I had the enclosed letter from Mrs Hepburn. I don't intend her to have the doll which is your portrait, so I shall not answer this note. Also I don't see why she should try to turn us out of the town. She talked to me after tea that day, and it seems she believes that Mitchka is your lover. I didn't say anything at all — except that it wasn't true. But she needn't be afraid of me. I don't want you to trouble yourself. But you may as well KNOW how things are.

JOHANNA Z. R.

The other letter was on his wife's well-known heavy paper, and in her well-known large, 'aristocratic' hand.

My dear Countess,

I wonder if there has been some mistake, or some misunderstanding. Four days ago you said you would send round that DOLL we spoke of, but I have seen no sign of it yet. I thought of calling at the studio, but did not wish to disturb the Baroness. I should be very much obliged if you could send the doll at once, as I do not feel easy while it is out of my possession. You may rely on having a cheque by return.

Our old family friend, Major-General Barlow, called on me yesterday, and we had a most interesting conversation on our Tommies, and the protection of their morals here. It seems we have full power to send away any person or persons deemed undesirable, with twenty-four hours' notice to leave. But of course all this is done as quietly and with the intention of causing as little scandal as possible.

Please let me have the doll by tomorrow, and perhaps some hint as to your future intentions.

With very best wishes from one who only seeks to be your friend. Yours very sincerely,

EVANGELINE HEPBURN.

Chapter 7

And then a dreadful thing happened: really a very dreadful thing. Hannele read of it in the evening newspaper of the town — the Abendblatt. Mitchka came rushing up with the paper at ten o'clock at night, just when Hannele was going to bed.

Mrs Hepburn had fallen out of her bedroom window, from the third floor of the hotel, down on to the pavement below, and was killed. She was dressing for dinner. And apparently she had in the morning washed a certain little camisole, and put it on the window-sill to dry. She must have stood on a chair, reaching for it when she fell out of the window. Her husband, who was in the dressing-room, heard a queer little noise, a sort of choking cry, and came into her room to see what it was. And she wasn't there. The window was open, and the chair by the window. He looked round, and thought she had left the room for a moment, so returned to his shaving. He was half-shaved when one of the maids rushed in. When he looked out of the window down into the street he fainted, and would have fallen too if the maid had not pulled him in in time.

The very next day the captain came back to his attic. Hannele did not know, until quite late at night when he tapped on her door. She knew his soft tap immediately.

'Won't you come over for a chat?' he said.

She paused for some moments before she answered. And then perhaps surprise made her agree: surprise and curiosity.

'Yes, in a minute,' she said, closing her door in his face.

She found him sitting quite still, not even smoking, in his quiet attic. He did not rise, but just glanced round with a faint smile. And she thought his face seemed different, more flexible. But in the half-light she could not tell. She sat at some little distance from him.

'I suppose you've heard,' he said.

'Yes.'

After a long pause, he resumed:

'Yes. It seems an impossible thing to have happened. Yet it HAS happened.'

Hannele's ears were sharp. But strain them as she might, she could not catch the meaning of his voice.

'A terrible thing. A VERY terrible thing,' she said.

'Yes.'

'Do you think she fell quite accidentally?' she said.

'Must have done. The maid was in just a minute before, and she seemed as happy as possible. I suppose reaching over that broad window-ledge, her brain must suddenly have turned. I can't imagine why she didn't call me. She could never bear even to look out of a high window. Turned her ill instantly if she saw a space below her. She used to say she couldn't really look at the moon, it made her feel as if she would fall down a dreadful height. She never dared to more than glance at it. She always had the feeling, I suppose, of the awful space beneath her, if she were on the moon.'

Hannele was not listening to his words, but to his voice. There was something a little automatic in what he said. But then that is always so when people have had a shock.

'It must have been terrible for you too,' she said.

'Ah, yes. At the time it was awful. Awful. I felt the smash right inside me, you know.'

'Awful!' she repeated.

'But now,' he said, 'I feel very strangely happy about it. I feel happy about it. I feel happy for her sake, if you can understand that. I feel she has got out of some great tension. I feel she's free now for the first time in her life. She was a gentle soul, and an original soul, but she was like a fairy who is condemned to live in houses and sit on furniture and all that, don't you know. It was never her nature.'

'No?' said Hannele, herself sitting in blank amazement.

'I always felt she was born in the wrong period — or on the wrong planet. Like some sort of delicate creature you take out of a tropical forest the moment it is born, and from the first moment teach it to perform tricks. You know what I mean. All her life she performed the tricks of life, clever little monkey she was at it too. Beat me into fits. But her own poor little soul, a sort of fairy soul, those queer Irish creatures, was cooped up inside her all her life, tombed in. There it was, tombed in, while she went through all the tricks of life that you have to go through if you are born today.'

'But,' stammered Hannele, 'what would she have done if she HAD been free?'

'Why, don't you see, there IS nothing for her to do in the world today. Take her language, for instance. She never ought to have been speaking English. I don't know what language she ought to have spoken. Because if you take the Irish language, they only learn it back from English. They think in English, and just put Irish words on top. But English was never her language. It bubbled off her lips, so to speak. And she had no other language. Like a starling that you've made talk from the very beginning, and so it can only shout these talking noises, don't you know. It can't whistle its own whistling to save its life.

Couldn't do it. It's lost it. All its own natural mode of expressing itself has collapsed, and it can only be artificial.'

There was a long pause.

'Would she have been wonderful, then, if she had been able to talk in some unknown language?' said Hannele jealously.

'I don't say she would have been wonderful. As a matter of fact, we think a talking starling is much more wonderful than an ordinary starling. I don't myself, but most people do. And she would have been a sort of starling. And she would have had her own language and her own ways. As it was, poor thing, she was always arranging herself and fluttering and chattering inside a cage. And she never knew she was in the cage, any more than we know we are inside our own skins.'

'But,' said Hannele, with a touch of mockery, 'how do you know you haven't made it all up — just to console yourself?'

'Oh, I've thought it long ago,' he said.

'Still,' she blurted, 'you may have invented it all — as a sort of consolation for — for — for your life.'

'Yes, I may,' he said. 'But I don't think so. It was her eyes. Did you ever notice her eyes? I often used to catch her eyes. And she'd be talking away, all the language bubbling off her lips. And her eyes were so clear and bright and different. Like a child's that is listening to something, and is going to be frightened. She was always listening — and waiting — for something else. I tell you what, she was exactly like that fairy in the Scotch song, who is in love with a mortal, and sits by the high road in terror waiting for him to come, and hearing the plovers and the curlews. Only nowadays motor-lorries go along the moor roads and the poor thing is struck unconscious, and carried into our world in a state of unconsciousness, and when she comes round, she tries to talk our language and behave as we behave, and she can't remember anything else, so she goes on and on, till she falls with a crash, back to her own world.'

Hannele was silent, and so was he.

'You loved her then?' she said at length.

'Yes. But in this way. When I was a boy I caught a bird, a black-cap, and I put it in a cage. And I loved that bird. I don't know why, but I loved it. I simply loved that bird. All the gorse, and the heather, and the rock, and the hot smell of yellow gorse blossom, and the sky that seemed to have no end to it, when I was a boy, everything that I almost was MAD with, as boys are, seemed to me to be in that little, fluttering black-cap. And it would peck its seed as if it didn't quite know what else to do; and look round about, and begin to sing. But in quite a few days it turned its head aside and died. Yes, it died. I never had the feeling again that I got from that black-cap when I was a boy — not until I saw her. And then I felt it all again. I felt it all again. And it was the same feeling. I knew, quite soon I knew, that she would die. She would peck her seed and look round in the cage just the same. But she would die in the end. Only it would last much longer. But she would die in the cage, like the black-cap.'

'But she loved the cage. She loved her clothes and her jewels. She must have loved her house and her furniture and all that with a perfect frenzy.'

'She did. She did. But like a child with playthings. Only they were big, marvellous playthings to her. Oh yes, she was never away from them. She never forgot her things — her trinkets and her furs and her furniture. She never got away from them for a minute. And everything in her mind was mixed up with them.'

'Dreadful!' said Hannele.

'Yes, it was dreadful,' he answered.

'Dreadful,' repeated Hannele.

'Yes, quite. Quite! And it got worse. And her way of talking got worse. As if it bubbled off her lips. But her eyes never lost their brightness, they never lost that faery look. Only I used to see fear in them. Fear of everything — even all the things she surrounded herself with. Just like my black-cap used to look out of his cage — so bright and sharp, and yet as if he didn't know that it was just the cage that was between him and the outside. He thought it was inside himself, the barrier. He thought it was part of his own nature to be shut in. And she thought it was part of her own nature. And so they both died.'

'What I can't see,' said Hannele, 'is what she would have done outside her cage. What other life could she have, except her bibelots and her furniture, and her talk?'

'Why, none. There IS no life outside for human beings.'

'Then there's nothing,' said Hannele.

'That's true. In a great measure, there's nothing.'

'Thank you,' said Hannele.

There was a long pause.

'And perhaps I was to blame. Perhaps I ought to have made some sort of a move. But I didn't know what to do. For my life, I didn't know what to do, except try to make her happy. She had enough money — and I didn't think it mattered if she shared it with me. I always had a garden — and the astronomy. It's been an immense relief to me watching the moon. It's been wonderful. Instead of looking inside the cage, as I did at my bird, or at her — I look right out — into freedom — into freedom.'

'The moon, you mean?' said Hannele.

'Yes, the moon.'

'And that's your freedom?'

'That's where I've found the greatest sense of freedom,' he said.

'Well, I'm not going to be jealous of the moon,' said Hannele at length.

'Why should you? It's not a thing to be jealous of.'

In a little while, she bade him good-night and left him.

Chapter 8

The chief thing that the captain knew, at this juncture, was that a hatchet had gone through the ligatures and veins that connected him with the people of his affection, and that he was left with the bleeding ends of all his vital human relationships. Why it should be so he did not know. But then one never can know the whys and the wherefores of one's passional changes.

He only knew that it was so. The emotional flow between him and all the people he knew and cared for was broken, and for the time being he was conscious only of the cleavage. The cleavage that had occurred between him and his fellow-men, the cleft that was now between him and them. It was not the fault of anybody or anything. He could neither reproach himself nor them. What had happened had been preparing for a long time. Now suddenly the cleavage. There had been a long, slow weaning away: and now this sudden silent rupture.

What it amounted to principally was that he did not want even to see Hannele. He did not want to think of her even. But neither did he want to see anybody else, or to think of anybody else. He shrank with a feeling almost of disgust from his friends and acquaintances, and their expressions of sympathy. It affected him with instantaneous disgust when anybody wanted to share emotions with him. He did not want to share emotions or feelings of any sort. He wanted to be by himself, essentially, even if he was moving about among other people.

So he went to England to settle his own affairs, and out of duty to see his children. He wished his children all the well in the world — everything except any emotional connexion with himself. He decided to take his girl away from the convent at once, and to put her into a jolly English school. His boy was all right where he was.

The captain had now an income sufficient to give him his independence, but not sufficient to keep up his wife's house. So he prepared to sell the house and most of the things in it. He decided also to leave the army as soon as he could be free. And he thought he would wander about for a time, till he came upon something he wanted.

So the winter passed, without his going back to Germany. He was free of the army. He drifted along, settling his affairs. They were of no very great importance. And all the time he never wrote once to Hannele. He could not get over his disgust that people insisted on his sharing their emotions. He could not bear their emotions, neither their activities. Other people might have all the emotions and feelings and earnestness and busy activities they liked. Quite nice even that they had such a multifarious commotion for themselves. But the moment they approached him to spread their feelings over him or to entangle him in their activities a helpless disgust came up in him, and until he could get away he felt sick, even physically.

This was no state of mind for a lover. He could not even think of Hannele. Anybody else he felt he need not think about. He was deeply, profoundly thankful that his wife was dead. It was an end of pity now; because, poor thing, she had escaped and gone her own way into the void, like a flown bird.

Chapter 9

Nevertheless, a man hasn't finished his life at forty. He may, however, have finished one great phase of his life.

And Alexander Hepburn was not the man to live alone. All our troubles, says somebody wise, come upon us because we cannot be alone. And that is all very well. We must all be ABLE to be alone, otherwise we are just victims. But when we ARE able to be alone, then we realize that the only thing to do is to start a new relationship with another — or even the same — human being. That people should all be stuck up apart, like so many telegraph-poles, is nonsense.

So with our dear captain. He had his convulsion into a sort of telegraph-pole isolation: which was absolutely necessary for him. But then he began to bud with a new yearning for — for what? For love?

It was a question he kept nicely putting to himself. And really, the nice young girls of eighteen or twenty attracted him very much: so fresh, so impulsive, and looking up to him as if he were something wonderful. If only he could have married two or three of them, instead of just one!

Love! When a man has no particular ambition, his mind turns back perpetually, as a needle towards the pole. That tiresome word Love. It means so many things. It meant the feeling he had had for his wife. He had loved her. But he shuddered at the thought of having to go through such love again. It meant also the feeling he had for the awfully nice young things he met here and there: fresh, impulsive girls ready to give all their hearts away. Oh yes, he could fall in love with half a dozen of them. But he knew he'd better not.

At last he wrote to Hannele: and got no answer. So he wrote to Mitchka and still got no answer. So he wrote for information — and there was none forthcoming, except that the two women had gone to Munich.

For the time being he left it at that. To him, Hannele did not exactly represent rosy love. Rather a hard destiny. He did not adore her. He did not feel one bit of adoration for her. As a matter of fact, not all the beauties and virtues of woman put together with all the gold in the

Indies would have tempted him into the business of adoration any more. He had gone on his knees once, vowing with faltering tones to try and make the adored one happy. And now — never again. Never.

The temptation this time was to be adored. One of those fresh young things would have adored him as if he were a god. And there was something VERY alluring about the thought. Very — very alluring. To be god-almighty in your own house, with a lovely young thing adoring you, and you giving off beams of bright effulgence like a Gloria! Who wouldn't be tempted: at the age of forty? And this was why he dallied.

But in the end he suddenly took the train to Munich. And when he got there he found the town beastly uncomfortable, the Bavarians rude and disagreeable, and no sign of the missing females, not even in the Café Stéphanie. He wandered round and round.

And then one day, oh heaven, he saw his doll in a shop window: a little art shop. He stood and stared quite spellbound.

'Well, if that isn't the devil,' he said. 'Seeing yourself in a shop window!'

He was so disgusted that he would not go into the shop.

Then, every day for a week did he walk down that little street and look at himself in the shop window. Yes, there he stood, with one hand in his pocket. And the figure had one hand in its pocket. There he stood, with his cap pulled rather low over his brow. And the figure had its cap pulled low over its brow. But, thank goodness, his own cap now was a civilian tweed. But there he stood, his head rather forward, gazing with fixed dark eyes. And himself in little, that wretched figure, stood there with its head rather forward, staring with fixed dark eyes. It was such a real little MAN that it fairly staggered him. The oftener he saw it, the more it staggered him. And the more he hated it. Yet it fascinated him, and he came again to look.

And it was always there. A lonely little individual lounging there with one hand in its pocket, and nothing to do, among the bric-à-brac and the bibelots. Poor devil, stuck so incongruously in the world. And yet losing none of his masculinity.

A male little devil, for all his forlornness. But such an air of isolation, or not-belonging. Yet taut and male, in his tartan trews. And what a situation to be in! — lounging with his back against a little Japanese lacquer cabinet, with a few old pots on his right hand and a tiresome brass ink-tray on his left, while pieces of not-very-nice filet lace hung their length up and down the background. Poor little devil: it was like a deliberate satire.

And then one day it was gone. There was the cabinet and the filet lace and the tiresome ink-stand tray: and the little gentleman wasn't there. The captain at once walked into the shop.

'Have you sold that doll? — that unknown soldier?' he added, without knowing quite what he was saying.

The doll was sold.

'Do you know who bought it?'

The girl looked at him very coldly, and did not know.

'I once knew the lady who made it. In fact, the doll was ME,' he said.

The girl now looked at him with sudden interest.

'Don't you think it was like me?' he said.

'Perhaps' — she began to smile.

'It was me. And the lady who made it was a friend of mine. Do you know her name?'

'Yes.'

'Gräfin zu Rassentlow,' he cried, his eyes shining.

'Oh yes. But her dolls are famous.'

'Do you know where she is? Is she in Munich?'

'That I don't know.'

'Could you find out?'

'I don't know. I can ask.'

'Or the Baroness von Prielau-Carolath.'

'The Baroness is dead.'

'Dead!'

'She was shot in a riot in Salzburg. They say a lover — '

'How do you know?'

'From the newspapers.'

'Dead! Is it possible. Poor Hannele.'

There was a pause.

'Well,' he said, 'if you would inquire about the address — I'll call again.'

Then he turned back from the door.

'By the way, do you mind telling me how much you sold the doll for?'

The girl hesitated. She was by no means anxious to give away any of her trade details. But at length she answered reluctantly:

'Five hundred marks.'

'So cheap,' he said.' Good-day. Then I will call again.'

Chapter 10

Then again he got a trace. It was in the Chit-Chat column of the Münchener Neue Zeitung: under Studio-Comments. 'Theodor Worpswede's latest picture is a still-life, containing an entertaining group of a doll, two sunflowers in a glass jar, and a poached egg on toast. The contrast between the three substances is highly diverting and instructive, and this is perhaps one of the most interesting of Worpswede's works. The doll, by the way, is one of the creations of our fertile Countess Hannele. It is the figure of an English, or rather Scottish, officer in the famous tartan trousers which, clinging closely to the legs of the lively Gaul, so shocked the eminent Julius Caesar and his cohorts. We, of course, are no longer shocked, but full of admiration for the creative genius of our dear Countess. The doll itself is a masterpiece, and has begotten another masterpiece in Theodor Worpswede's Still-life. We have heard, by the way, a rumour of Countess zu Rassentlow's engagement. Apparently the Herr Regierungsrat von Poldi, of that most beautiful of summer resorts, Kaprun, in the Tyrol, is the fortunate man —'

Chapter 11

The captain bought the Still-life. This new version of himself along with the poached egg and the sunflowers was rather frightening. So he packed up for Austria, for Kaprun, with his picture, and had a fight to get the beastly thing out of Germany, and another fight to get it into Austria. Fatigued and furious he arrived in Salzburg, seeing no beauty in anything. Next day he was in Kaprun.

It was an elegant and fashionable watering-place before the war: a lovely little lake in the midst of the Alps, an old Tyrolese town on the water-side, green slopes sheering up opposite, and away beyond a glacier. It was still crowded and still elegant. But alas, with a broken, bankrupt, desperate elegance, and almost empty shops.

The captain felt rather dazed. He found himself in an hotel full of Jews of the wrong, rich sort, and wondered what next. The place was beautiful, but the life wasn't.

Chapter 12

The Herr Regierungsrat was not at first sight prepossessing. He was approaching fifty, and had gone stout and rather loose, as so many men of his class and race do. Then he wore one of those dreadful full-bottom coats, a kind of poor relation to our full-skirted frock-coat: it would best be described as a family coat. It flapped about him as he walked, and he looked at first glance lower middle class.

But he wasn't. Of course, being in office in the collapsed Austria, he was a republican. But by nature he was a monarchist, nay, an imperialist, as every true Austrian is. And he was a true Austrian. And as such he was much finer and subtler than he looked. As one got used to him, his rather fat face, with its fine nose and slightly bitter, pursed mouth, came to have a resemblance to the busts of some of the late Roman emperors. And as one was with him, one came gradually to realize that out of all his baggy bourgeois appearance came something of a grand geste. He could not help it. There was something sweeping and careless about his soul: big, rather assertive, and ill-bred-seeming; but, in fact, not ill-bred at all, only a little bitter and a good deal indifferent to his surroundings. He looked at first sight so common and parvenu. And then one had to realize that he was a member of a big, old empire, fallen into a sort of epicureanism, and a little bitter. There was no littleness, no meanness, and no real coarseness. But he was a great talker, and relentless towards his audience.

Hannele was attracted to him by his talk. He began as soon as dinner appeared: and he went on, carrying the decanter and the wine-glass with him out on to the balcony of the villa, over the lake, on and on until midnight. The summer night was still and warm: the lake lay deep and full, and the old town twinkled away across. There was the faintest tang of snow in the air, from the great glacier-peaks that were hidden in the night opposite. Sometimes a boat with a lantern twanged a guitar. The clematis flowers were quite black, like leaves, dangling from the terrace.

It was so beautiful, there in the very heart of the Tyrol. The hotels glittered with lights: electric light was still cheap. There seemed a fullness and a loveliness in the night. And yet for some reason it was all terrible and devastating: the life-spirit seemed to be squirming, bleeding all the time.

And on and on talked the Herr Regierungsrat, with all the witty volubility of the more versatile Austrian. He was really very witty, very human, and with a touch of salty cynicism that reminded one of a real old Roman of the Empire. That subtle stoicism, that unsentimental epicureanism, that kind of reckless hopelessness, of course, fascinated the women. And particularly Hannele. He talked on and on — about his work before the war, when he held an important post and was one of the governing class — then about the war — then about the hopelessness of the present: and in it all there seemed a bigness, a carelessness based on indifference and hopelessness that laughed at its very self. The real old Austria had always fascinated Hannele. As represented in the witty, bitter-indifferent Herr Regierungsrat it carried her away.

And he, of course, turned instinctively to her, talking in his rapid, ceaseless fashion, with a laugh and a pause to drink and a new start taken. She liked the sound of his Austrian speech: its racy carelessness, its salty indifference to standards of correctness. Oh yes, here was the grand geste still lingering.

He turned his large breast towards her, and made a quick gesture with his fat, well-shapen hand, blurted out another subtle, rough-seeming romance, pursed his mouth, and emptied his glass once more. Then he looked at his half-forgotten cigar and started again.

There was something almost boyish and impulsive about him: the way he turned to her, and the odd way he seemed to open his big breast to her. And again he seemed almost eternal, sitting there in his chair with knees planted apart. It was as if he would never rise again, but would remain sitting for ever, and talking. He seemed as if he had no legs, save to sit with. As if to stand on his feet and walk would not be natural to him.

Yet he rose at last, and kissed her hand with the grand gesture that France or Germany have never acquired: carelessness, profound indifference to other people's standards, and then such a sudden stillness, as he bent and kissed her hand. Of course she felt a queen in exile.

And perhaps it is more dangerous to feel yourself a queen in exile than a queen in situ. She fell in love with him, with this large, stout, loose widower of fifty, with two children. He had no money except some Austrian money that was worth nothing outside Austria. He could not even go to Germany. There he was, fixed in this hollow in the middle of the Tyrol.

But he had an ambition still, old Roman of the decadence that he was. He had year by year and without making any fuss collected the material for a very minute and thorough history of his own district: the Chiemgau and the Pinzgau. Hannele found that his fund of information on this subject was inexhaustible, and his intelligence was so delicate, so human, and his scope seemed so wide, that she felt a touch of reverence for him. He wanted to write this history. And she wanted to help him.

For, of course, as things were he would never write it. He was Regierungsrat: that is, he was the petty local governor of his town and immediate district. The Amthaus was a great old building, and there young ladies in high heels flirted among masses of papers with bare-kneed young gentlemen in Tyrolese costume, and occasionally they parted to take a pleasant, interesting attitude and write a word or two, after which they fluttered together for a little more interesting diversion. It was extraordinary how many finely built, handsome young people of an age fitted for nothing but love-affairs ran the governmental business of this department. And the Herr Regierungsrat sailed in and out of the big, old room, his wide coat flying like wings and making the papers flutter, his rather wine-reddened, old-Roman face smiling with its bitter look. And of course it was a witticism he uttered first, even if Hungary was invading the frontier or cholera was in Vienna.

When he was on his legs, he walked nimbly, briskly, and his coat-bottoms always flew. So he waved through the town, greeting somebody at every few strides and grinning, and yet with a certain haughty reserve. Oh yes, there was a certain salty hauteur about him which made the people trust him. And he spoke the vernacular so racily.

Hannele felt she would like to marry him. She would like to be near him. She would like him to write his history. She would like him to make her feel a queen in exile. No one had ever QUITE kissed her hand as he kissed it: with that sudden stillness and strange, chivalric abandon of himself. How he would abandon himself to her! — terribly — wonderfully — perhaps a little horribly. His wife, whom he had married late, had died after seven years of marriage. Hannele could understand that too. One or the other must die.

She became engaged. But something made her hesitate before marriage. Being in Austria was like being on a wrecked ship that MUST sink after a certain short length of time. And marrying the Herr Regierungsrat was like marrying the doomed captain of the doomed ship. The sense of fatality was part of the attraction.

And yet she hesitated. The summer weeks passed. The strangers flooded in and crowded the town, and ate up the food like locusts. People no longer counted the paper money, they weighed it by the kilogram. Peasants stored it in a corner of the meal-bin, and mice came and chewed holes in it. Nobody knew where the next lot of food was going to come from: yet it always came. And the lake teemed with bathers. When the captain arrived he looked with amazement on the crowds of strapping, powerful fellows who bathed all day long, magnificent blond flesh of men and women. No wonder the old Romans stood in astonishment before the huge blond limbs of the savage Germana.

Well, the life was like a madness. The hotels charged fifteen hundred kronen a day: the women, old and young, paraded in the peasant costume, in flowery cotton dresses with gaudy, expensive silk aprons: the men wore the Tyrolese costume, bare knees and little short jackets. And for the men, the correct thing was to have the leathern hose and the blue linen jacket as old as possible. If you had a hole in your leathern seat, so much the better.

Everything so physical. Such magnificent naked limbs and naked bodies, and in the streets, in the hotels, everywhere, bare, white arms of women and bare, brown, powerful knees and thighs of men. The sense of flesh everywhere, and the endless ache of flesh. Even in the peasants who rowed across the lake, standing and rowing with a slow, heavy, gondolier motion at the one curved oar, there was the same endless ache of physical yearning.

Chapter 13

It was August when Alexander met Hannele. She was walking under a chintz parasol, wearing a dress of blue cotton with little red roses, and a red silk apron. She had no hat, her arms were bare and soft, and she had white stockings under her short dress. The Herr Regierungsrat was at her side, large, nimble, and laughing with a new witticism.

Alexander, in a light summer suit and Panama hat, was just coming out of the bank, shoving twenty thousand kronen into his pocket. He saw her coming across from the Amtsgericht, with the Herr Regierungsrat at her side, across the space of sunshine. She was laughing, and did not notice him.

She did not notice till he had taken off his hat and was saluting her. Then what she saw was the black, smooth, shining head, and she went pale. His black, smooth, close head — and all the blue Austrian day seemed to shrivel before her eyes.

'How do you do, Countess! I hoped I should meet you.'

She heard his slow, sad-clanging, straying voice again, and she pressed her hand with the umbrella stick against her breast. She had forgotten it — forgotten his peculiar, slow voice. And now it seemed like a noise that sounds in the silence of night. Ah, how difficult it was, that suddenly the world could split under her eyes, and show this darkness inside. She wished he had not come.

She presented him to the Herr Regierungsrat, who was stiff and cold. She asked where the captain was staying. And then, not knowing what else to say, she said:

'Won't you come to tea?'

She was staying in a villa across the lake. Yes, he would come to tea.

He went. He hired a boat and a man to row him across. It was not far. There stood the villa, with its brown balconies one above the other, the bright red geraniums and white geraniums twinkling all round, the trees of purple clematis tumbling at one corner. All the green window doors were open: but nobody about. In the little garden by the water's edge the rose trees were tall and lank, drawn up by the dark green trees of the background. A white table with chairs and garden seats stood under — the shadow of a big willow tree, and a hammock with cushions swung just behind. But no one in sight. There was a little landing bridge on to the garden: and a fairly large boat-house at the garden end.

The captain was not sure that the boat-house belonged to the villa. Voices were shouting and laughing from the water's surface, bathers swimming. A tall, naked youth with a little red cap on his head and a tiny red loin-cloth round his slender young hips was standing on the steps of the boat-house calling to the three women who were swimming near. The dark-haired woman with the white cap swam up to the steps and caught the boy by the ankle. He cried and laughed and remonstrated, and poked her in the breast with his foot.

'Nein, nein, Hardu!' she cried as he tickled her with his toe. 'Hardu! Hardu! Hör' auf! — Leave off!' — and she fell with a crash back into the water. The youth laughed a loud, deep laugh of a lad whose voice is newly broken.

'Was macht er dann?' cried a voice from the waters. 'What is he doing?' It was a dark-skinned girl swimming swiftly, her big dark eyes watching amused from the water surface.

'Jetzt Hardu hör' auf. Nein. Jetzt ruhig! Now leave off! Now be quiet.' And the dark-skinned woman was climbing out in the sunshine onto the pale, raw-wood steps of the boathouse, the water glistening on her dark-blue, stockinette, soft-moulded back and loins: while the boy, with his foot stretched out, was trying to push her back into the water. She clambered out, however, and sat on the steps in the sun, panting slightly. She was dark and attractive-looking, with a mature beautiful figure, and handsome, strong woman's legs.

In the garden appeared a black-and-white maid-servant with a tray.

'Kaffee, gnädige Frau!'

The voice came so distinct over the water.

'Hannele! Hannele! Kaffee!' called the woman on the steps of the bathing-house.

'Tante Hannele! Kaffee!' called the dark-eyed girl, turning round in the water, then swimming for home.

'Kaffee! Kaffee!' roared the youth, in anticipation.

'Ja — a! Ich kom — mm,' sang Hannele's voice from the water.

The dark-eyed girl, her hair tied up in a silk bandana, had reached the steps and was climbing out, a slim young fish in her close dark suit. The three stood clustered on the steps, the elder woman with one arm over the naked shoulders of the youth, the other arm over the shoulders of the girl. And all in chorus sang:

'Hannele! Hannele! Hannele! Wir warten auf dich.'

The boatman had left off rowing, and the boat was drifting slowly in. The family became quiet, because of the intrusion. The attractive-looking woman turned and picked up her blue bath-robe, of a mid-blue colour that became her. She swung it round her as if it were an opera cloak. The youth stared at the boat.

The captain was watching Hannele. With a white kerchief tied round her silky, brownish hair, she was swimming home. He saw her white shoulders and her white, wavering legs below in the clear water. Round the boat fishes were suddenly jumping.

The three on the steps beyond stood silent, watching the intruding boat with resentment. The boatman twisted his head round and watched them. The captain, who was facing them, watched Hannele. She swam slowly and easily up, caught the rail of the steps, and stooping forward, climbed slowly out of the water. Her legs were large and flashing white and looked rich, the rich, white thighs with the blue veins behind, and the full, rich softness of her sloping loins.

'Ach! Schön! 'S war schön! Das Wasser ist gut,' her voice was heard, half singing as she took her breath. 'It was lovely.'

'Heiss,' said the woman above. 'Zu warm. Too warm.'

The youth made way for Hannele, who drew herself erect at the top of the steps, looking round, panting a little and putting up her hands to the knot of her kerchief on her head. Her legs were magnificent and white.

'Kuck de Leut, die da bleiben,' said the woman in the blue wrap, in a low voice. 'Look at the people stopping there.'

'Ja!' said Hannele negligently. Then she looked. She started as if in fear, looked round, as if to run away, looked back again, and met the eyes of the captain, who took off his hat.

She cried in a loud, frightened voice:

'Oh, but — I thought it was TOMORROW!'

'No — today,' came the quiet voice of the captain over the water.

'TODAY! Are you sure?' she cried, calling to the boat.

'Quite sure. But we'll make it tomorrow if you like,' he said.

'Today! Today!' she repeated in bewilderment.' No! Wait a minute.' And she ran into the boat-house.

'Was ist es?' asked the dark woman, following her. 'What is it?'

'A friend — a visitor — Captain Hepburn,' came Hannele's voice.

The boatman now rowed slowly to the landing-stage. The dark woman, huddled in her blue wrap as in an opera-cloak, walked proudly and unconcernedly across the background of the garden and up the steps to the first balcony. Hannele, her feet slip-slopping in loose slippers, clutching an old yellow wrap round her, came to the landing-stage and shook hands.

'I am so sorry. It is so stupid of me. I was sure it was tomorrow,' she said.

'No, it was today. But I wish for your sake it had been tomorrow,' he replied.

'No. No. It doesn't matter. You won't mind waiting a minute, will you? You mustn't be angry with me for being so stupid.'

So she went away, the heelless slippers flipping up to her naked heels. Then the big-eyed, dusky girl stole into the house: and then the naked youth, who went with sang-froid. He would make a fine, handsome man: and he knew it.

Chapter 14

Hepburn and Hannele were to make a small excursion to the glacier which stood there always in sight, coldly grinning in the sky. The weather had been very hot, but this morning there were loose clouds in the sky. The captain rowed over the lake soon after dawn. Hannele stepped into the little craft, and they pulled back to the town. There was a wind ruffling the water, so that the boat leaped and chuckled. The glacier, in a recess among the folded mountains, looked cold and angry. But morning was very sweet in the sky, and blowing very sweet with a faint scent of the second hay from the low lands at the head of the lake. Beyond stood naked grey rock like a wall of mountains, pure rock, with faint, thin slashes of snow. Yesterday it had rained on the lake. The sun was going to appear from behind the Breitsteinhorn, the sky with its clouds floating in blue light and yellow radiance was lovely and cheering again. But dark clouds seemed to spout up from the Pinzgau valley. And once across the lake, all was shadow, when the water no longer gave back the sky-morning.

The day was a feast day, a holiday. Already so early three young men from the mountains were bathing near the steps of the

Badeanstalt. Handsome, physical fellows, with good limbs rolling and swaying in the early morning water. They seemed to enjoy it too. But to Hepburn it was always as if a dark wing were stretched in the sky, over these mountains, like a doom. And these three young, lusty, naked men swimming and rolling in the shadow.

Hepburn's was the first boat stirring. He made fast in the hotel boat-house, and he and Hannele went into the little town. It was deep in shadow, though the light of the sky, curdled with cloud, was bright overhead. But dark and chill and heavy lay the shadow in the black-and-white town, like a sediment.

The shops were all shut, but peasants from the hills were already strolling about in their holiday dress: the men in their short leather trousers, like football drawers, and bare brown knees and great boots: their little grey jackets faced with green, and their green hats with the proud chamois-brush behind. They seemed to stray about like lost souls, and the proud chamois-brush behind their hats, this proud, cocky, perking-up tail, like a mountain-buck with his tail up, was belied by the lost-soul look of the men, as they loitered about with their hands shoved in the front pockets of their trousers. Some women also were creeping about: peasant women, in the funny little black hats that had thick gold under the brim and long black streamers of ribbon, broad, black, water-wave ribbon starting from a bow under the brim behind and streaming right to the bottom of the skirt. These women, in their thick, dark dresses with tight bodices and massive, heavy, full skirts, and bright or dark aprons, strode about with the heavy stride of the mountain women, the heavy, quick, forward-leaning motion. They were waiting for the town-day to begin.

Hepburn had a knapsack on his back, with food for the day. But bread was wanting. They found the door of the bakery open, and got a loaf: a long, hot loaf of pure white bread, beautifully sweet bread. It cost seventy kronen. To Hepburn it was always a mystery where this exquisite bread came from, in a lost land.

In the little square where the clock stood were bunches of people, and a big motor-omnibus, and a motor-car that would hold about eight people. Hepburn had paid his seven hundred kronen for the two tickets. Hannele tied up her head in a thin scarf and put on her thick coat. She and Hepburn sat in front by the peaked driver. And at seven o'clock away went the car, swooping out of the town, past the handsome old Tyrolese Schloss, or manor, black-and-white, with its little black spires pricking up, past the station, and under the trees by the lakeside. The road was not good, but they ran at a great speed, out past the end of the lake, where the reeds grew, out into the open valley mouth, where the mountains opened in two clefts. It was cold in the car. Hepburn buttoned himself up to the throat and pulled his hat down on his ears. Hannele's scarf fluttered. She sat without saying anything, erect, her face fine and keen, watching ahead. From the deep Pinzgau Valley came the river roaring and raging, a glacier river of pale, seething ice-water. Over went the car, over the log bridge, darting towards the great slopes opposite. And then a sudden immense turn, a swerve under the height of the mountain-side, and again a darting lurch forward, under the pear trees of the high-road, past the big old ruined castle that so magnificently watched the valley mouth, and the foaming river; on, rushing under the huge roofs of the balconied peasant houses of a village, then swinging again to take another valley mouth, there where a little village clustered all black and white on a knoll, with a white church that had a black steeple, and a white castle with black spires, and clustering, ample black-and-white houses of the Tyrol. There is a grandeur even in the peasant houses, with their great wide passage halls where the swallows build, and where one could build a whole English cottage.

So the motor-car darted up this new, narrow, wilder, more sinister valley. A herd of almost wild young horses, handsome reddish things, burst around the car, and one great mare with full flanks went crashing up the road ahead, her heels flashing to the car, while her foal whinneyed and screamed from behind. But no, she could not turn from the road. On and on she crashed, forging ahead, the car behind her. And then at last she did swerve aside, among the thin alder trees by the wild riverbed.

'If it isn't a cow, it's a horse,' said the driver, who was thin and weaselish and silent, with his ear-flaps over his ears.

But the great mare had shaken herself in a wild swerve, and screaming and whinneying was plunging back to her foal. Hannele had been frightened.

The car rushed on, through water-meadows, along a naked, white bit of mountain road. Ahead was a darkness of mountain front and pine trees. To the right was the stony, furious, lion-like river, tawny-coloured here, and the slope up beyond. But the road for the moment was swinging fairly level through the stunned water-meadows of the savage valley. There were gates to open, and Hepburn jumped down to open them, as if he were the footboy. The heavy Jews of the wrong sort, seated behind, of course did not stir.

At a house on a knoll the driver sounded his horn, and out rushed children crying Papa! Papa! — then a woman with a basket. A few brief words from the weaselish man, who smiled with warm, manly blue eyes at his children, then the car leaped forward. The whole bearing of the man was so different when he was looking at his own family. He could not even say thank you when Hepburn opened the gates. He hated and even despised his human cargo of middle-class people. Deep, deep is class hatred, and it begins to swallow all human feeling in its abyss. So, stiff, silent, thin, capable, and neuter towards his fares, sat the little driver with the flaps over his ears, and his thin nose cold.

The car swept round, suddenly, into the trees: and into the ravine. The river shouted at the bottom of a gulf. Bristling pine trees stood around. The air was black and cold and forever sunless. The motor-car rushed on, in this blackness under the rock-walls and the fir trees.

Then it suddenly stopped. There was a huge motor-omnibus ahead, drab and enormous-looking. Tourists and trippers of last night coming back from the glacier. It stood like a great rock. And the smaller motor-car edged past, tilting into the rock gutter under the face of stone.

So, after a while of this valley of the shadow of death, lurching in steep loops upwards, the motor-car scrambling wonderfully, struggling past trees and rock upwards, at last they came to the end. It was a huge inn or tourist hotel of brown wood: and here the road ended in a little wide bay surrounded and overhung by trees. Beyond was a garage and a bridge over a roaring river: and always the overhung darkness of trees and the intolerable steep slopes immediately above.

Hannele left her big coat. The sky looked blue above the gloom. They set out across the hollow-sounding bridge, over the everlasting mad rush of ice-water, to the immediate upslope of the path, under dark trees. But a little old man in a sort of sentry-box wanted fifty or sixty kronen: apparently for the upkeep of the road, a sort of toll.

The other tourists were coming — some stopping to have a drink first. The second omnibus had not yet arrived. Hannele and Hepburn were the first two, treading slowly up that dark path, under the trees. The grasses hanging on the rock face were still dewy. There were a few wild raspberries, and a tiny tuft of bilberries with black berries here and there, and a few tufts of unripe cranberries. The many hundreds of tourists who passed up and down did not leave much to pick. Some mountain harebells, like bells of blue water, hung coldly glistening in their darkness. Sometimes the hairy mountain-bell, pale-blue and bristling, stood alone, curving his head right down, stiff and taut. There was an occasional big, moist, lolling daisy.

So the two climbed slowly up the steep ledge of a road. This valley was just a mountain cleft, cleft sheer in the hard, living rock, with black trees like hair flourishing in this secret, naked place of the earth. At the bottom of the open wedge for ever roared the rampant, insatiable water. The sky from above was like a sharp wedge forcing its way into the earth's cleavage, and that eternal ferocious water was like the steel edge of the wedge, the terrible tip biting in into the rocks' intensity. Who could have thought that the soft sky of light, and the soft foam of water could thrust and penetrate into the dark, strong earth? But so it was. Hannele and Hepburn, toiling up the steep little ledge of a road that hung half-way down the gulf, looked back, time after time, back down upon the brown timbers and shingle roofs of the hotel, that now, away below, looked damp and wedged in like boulders. Then back at the next tourists struggling up. Then down at the water, that rushed like a beast of prey. And then, as they rose higher, they looked up also at the livid great sides of rock, livid, bare rock that sloped from the sky-ridge in a hideous sheer swerve downwards.

In his heart of hearts Hepburn hated it. He hated it, he loathed it, it seemed almost obscene, this livid, naked slide of rock, unthinkably huge and massive, sliding down to this gulf where bushes grew like hair in the darkness and water roared. Above, there were thin slashes of snow.

So the two climbed slowly on, up the eternal side of that valley, sweating with the exertion. Sometimes the sun, now risen high, shone full on their side of the gulley. Tourists were trickling downhill too: two maidens with bare arms and bare heads and huge boots: men tourists with great knapsacks and edelweiss in their hats: giving Bergheil for a greeting. But the captain said Good-day. He refused this Bergheil business. People swarming touristy on these horrible mountains made him feel almost sick.

He and Hannele also were not in good company together. There was a sort of silent hostility between them. She hated the effort of climbing; but the high air, the cold in the air, the savage cat-howling sound of the water, those awful flanks of livid rock, all this thrilled and excited her to another sort of savageness. And he, dark, rather slender and feline, with something of the physical suavity of a delicate-footed race, he hated beating his way up the rock, he hated the sound of the water, it frightened him, and the high air hit him in the chest, like a viper.

'Wonderful! Wonderful!' she cried, taking great breaths in her splendid chest.

'Yes. And horrible. Detestable,' he said.

She turned with a flash, and the high strident sound of the mountain in her voice.

'If you don't like it,' she said, rather jeering, 'why ever did you come?'

'I had to try,' he said.

'And if you don't like it,' she said, 'why should you try to spoil it for me?'

'I hate it,' he answered.

They were climbing more into the height, more into the light, into the open, in the full sun. The valley cleft was sinking below them. Opposite was only the sheer, livid slide of the naked rock, tipping from the pure sky. At a certain angle they could see away beyond the lake lying far off and small, the wall of those other rocks like a curtain of stone, dim and diminished to the horizon. And the sky with curdling clouds and blue sunshine intermittent.

'Wonderful, wonderful, to be high up,' she said, breathing great breaths.

'Yes,' he said. 'It IS wonderful. But very detestable. I want to live near the sea-level. I am no mountain-topper.'

'Evidently not,' she said.

'Bergheil!' cried a youth with bare arms and bare chest, bare head, terrific fanged boots, a knapsack and an alpenstock, and all the bronzed wind and sun of the mountain snow in his skin and his faintly bleached hair. With his great heavy knapsack, his rumpled thick stockings, his ghastly fanged boots, Hepburn found him repulsive.

'Guten Tag' he answered coldly.

'Gruss Gott,' said Hannele.

And the young Tannhäuser, the young Siegfried, this young Balder beautiful strode climbing down the rocks, marching and swinging with his alpenstock. And immediately after the youth came a maiden, with hair on the wind and her shirt-breast open, striding in corduroy breeches, rumpled worsted stockings, thick boots, a knapsack and an alpenstock. She passed without greeting. And our pair stopped in angry silence and watched her dropping down the mountain-side.

Chapter 15

Ah, well, everything comes to an end, even the longest up-climb. So, after much sweat and effort and crossness, Hepburn and Hannele emerged on to the rounded bluff where the road wound out of that hideous great valley cleft into upper regions. So they emerged more on the level, out of the trees as out of something horrible, on to a naked, great bank of rock and grass.

'Thank the Lord!' said Hannele.

So they trudged on round the bluff, and then in front of them saw what is always, always wonderful, one of those shallow, upper valleys, naked, where the first waters are rocked. A flat, shallow, utterly desolate valley, wide as a wide bowl under the sky, with rock slopes and grey stone-slides and precipices all round, and the zig-zag of snow-stripes and ice-roots descending, and then rivers, streams and rivers rushing from many points downwards, down out of the ice-roots and the snow-dagger-points, waters rushing in newly-liberated frenzy downwards, down in waterfalls and cascades and threads, down into the wide, shallow bed of the valley, strewn with rocks and stones innumerable, and not a tree, not a visible bush.

Only, of course, two hotels or restaurant places. But these no more than low, sprawling, peasant-looking places lost among the stones, with stones on their roofs so that they seemed just a part of the valley bed. There was the valley, dotted with rock and rolled-down stone, and these two house-places, and woven with innumerable new waters, and one hoarse stone-tracked river in the desert, and the thin road-track winding along the desolate flat, past first one house, then the other, over one stream, then another, on to the far rock-face above which the glacier seemed to loll like some awful great tongue put out.

'Ah, it is wonderful!' he said, as if to himself.

And she looked quickly at his face, saw the queer, blank, sphinx-look with which he gazed out beyond himself. His eyes were black and set, and he seemed so motionless, as if he were eternal facing these upper facts.

She thrilled with triumph. She felt he was overcome.

'It IS wonderful,' she said.

'Wonderful. And forever wonderful,' he said.

'Ah, in WINTER— ' she cried.

His face changed, and he looked at her.

'In winter you couldn't get up here,' he said.

They went on. Up the slopes cattle were feeding: came that isolated tong-tong-tong of cow-bells, dropping like the slow clink of ice on the arrested air. The sound always woke in him a primeval, almost hopeless melancholy. Always made him feel navré. He looked round. There was no tree, no bush, only great grey rocks and pale boulders scattered in place of trees and bushes. But yes, clinging on one side like a dark, close beard were the alpenrose shrubs.

'In May,' he said, 'that side there must be all pink with alpenroses.'

'I MUST come. I MUST come!' she cried.

There were tourists dotted along the road: and two tiny low carts drawn by silky, long-eared mules. These carts went right down to meet the motor-cars, and to bring up provisions for the Glacier Hotel: for there was still another big hotel ahead. Hepburn was happy in that upper valley, that first rocking cradle of early water. He liked to see the great fangs and slashes of ice and snow thrust down into the rock, as if the ice had bitten into the flesh of the earth. And from the fang-tips the hoarse water crying its birth-cry, rushing down.

By the turfy road and under the rocks were many flowers: wonderful harebells, big and cold and dark, almost black, and seeming like purple-dark ice: then little tufts of tiny pale-blue bells, as if some fairy frog had been blowing spume-bubbles out of the ice: then the bishops-crosier of the stiff, bigger, hairy mountain-bell: then many stars of pale-lavender gentian, touched with earth colour: and then monkshood, yellow, primrose yellow monkshood and sudden places full of dark monkshood. That dark-blue, black-blue, terrible colour of the strange rich monkshood made Hepburn look and look and look again. How did the ice come by that lustrous blue-purple intense darkness? — and by that royal poison? — that laughing-snake gorgeousness of much monkshood.

Chapter 16

By one of the loud streams, under a rock in the sun, with scented minty or thyme flowers near, they sat down to eat some lunch. It was about eleven o'clock. A thin bee went in and out the scented flowers and the eyebright. The water poured with all the lust and greed of unloosed water over the stones. He took a cupful for Hannele, bright and icy, and she mixed it with the red Hungarian wine.

Down the road strayed the tourists like pilgrims, and at the closed end of the valley they could be seen, quite tiny, climbing the cut-out road that went up like a stairway. Just by their movements you perceived them. But on the valley-bed they went like rolling stones, little as stones. A very elegant mule came stepping by, following a middle-aged woman in tweeds and a tall, high-browed man in knickerbockers. The mule was drawing a very amusing little cart, a chair, rather like a round office-chair upholstered in red velvet, and mounted on two wheels. The red velvet had gone gold and orange and like fruit-juice, being old: really a lovely colour. And the muleteer, a little shabby creature, waddled beside excitedly.

'Ach' cried Hannele, 'that looks almost like before the war: almost as peaceful.'

'Except that the chair is too shabby, and that they all feel exceptional,' he remarked.

There in that upper valley there was no sense of peace. The rush of the waters seemed like weapons, and the tourists all seemed in a sort of frenzy, in a frenzy to be happy, or to be thrilled. It was a feeling that desolated the heart.

The two sat in the changing sunshine under their rock, with the mountain flowers scenting the snow-bitter air, and they ate their eggs and sausage and cheese, and drank the bright-red Hungarian wine. It seemed lovely: almost like before the war: almost the same feeling of eternal holiday, as if the world was made for man's everlasting holiday. But not quite. Never again quite the same. The world is not made for man's everlasting holiday.

As Alexander was putting the bread back into his shoulder-sack, he exclaimed:

'Oh, look here!'

She looked, and saw him drawing out a flat package wrapped in paper: evidently a picture.

'A picture!' she cried.

He unwrapped the thing and handed it to her. It was Theodor Worpswede's Stilleben: not very large, painted on a board.

Hannele looked at it and went pale.

'It's GOOD,' she cried, in an equivocal tone.

'Quite good,' he said.

'Especially the poached egg,' she said.

'Yes, the poached egg is almost living.'

'But where did you find it?'

'Oh, I found it in the artist's studio.' And he told her how he had traced her.

'How extraordinary!' she cried. 'But why did you buy it?'

'I don't quite know.'

'Did you LIKE it?'

'No, not quite that.'

'You could NEVER hang it up.'

'No, never,' he said.

'But do you think it is good as a work of art?'

'I think it is quite clever as a painting. I don't like the spirit of it, of course. I'm too catholic for that.'

'No. No,' she faltered. 'It's rather horrid really. That's why I wonder why you bought it.'

'Perhaps to prevent anyone else's buying it,' he said.

'Do you mind very much, then?' she asked.

'No, I don't mind very much. I didn't quite like it that you sold the doll,' he said.

'I needed the money,' she said quietly.

'Oh, quite.'

There was a pause for some moments.

'I felt you'd sold ME,' she said, quiet and savage.

'When?'

'When your wife appeared. And when you DISAPPEARED.'

Again there was a pause: his pause this time.

'I did write to you,' he said.

'When?'

'Oh — March, I believe.'

'Oh yes. I had that letter.' Her voice was just as quiet, and even savager.

So there was a pause that belonged to both of them. Then she rose.

'I want to be going,' she said. 'We shall never get to the glacier at this rate.'

He packed up the picture, slung on his knapsack, and they set off. She stooped now and then to pick the starry, earth-lavender gentians from the roadside. As they passed the second of the valley hotels, they saw the man and wife sitting at a little table outside eating bread and cheese, while the mule-chair with its red velvet waited aside on the grass. They passed a whole grove of black-purple nightshade on the left, and some long, low cattle-huts which, with the stones on their roofs, looked as if they had grown up as stones grow in such places through the grass. In the wild, desert place some black pigs were snouting.

So they wound into the head of the valley, and saw the steep face ahead, and high up, like vapour or foam dripping from the fangs of a beast, waterfalls vapouring down from the deep fangs of ice. And there was one end of the glacier, like a great bluey-white fur just slipping over the slope of the rock.

As the valley closed in again the flowers were very lovely, especially the big, dark, icy bells, like harebells, that would sway so easily, but which hung dark and with that terrible motionlessness of upper mountain flowers. And the road turned to get on to the long slant in the cliff face, where it climbed like a stair. Slowly, slowly the two climbed up. Now again they saw the valley below, behind. The mule-chair was coming, hastening, the lady seated tight facing backwards, as the chair faced, and wrapped in rugs. The tall, fair, middle-aged husband in knickerbockers strode just behind, bare-headed.

Alexander and Hannele climbed slowly, slowly up the slant, under the dripping rock-face where the white and veined flowers of the grass of Parnassus still rose straight and chilly in the shadow, like water which had taken on itself white flower-flesh. Above they saw the slipping edge of the glacier, like a terrible great paw, bluey. And from the skyline dark grey clouds were fuming up, fuming up as if breathed black and icily out from some ice-cauldron.

'It is going to rain,' said Alexander.

'Not much,' said Hannele shortly.

'I hope not,' said he.

And still she would not hurry up that steep slant, but insisted on standing to look. So the dark, ice-black clouds fumed solid, and the rain began to fly on a cold wind. The mule-chair hastened past, the lady sitting comfortably with her back to the mule, a little pheasant-trimming in her tweed hat, while her Tannhäuser husband reached for his dark, cape-frilled mantle.

Alexander had his dust-coat, but Hannele had nothing but a light knitted jersey-coat, such as women wear indoors. Over the hollow crest above came the cold, steel rain. They pushed on up the slope. From behind came another mule, and a little old man hurrying, and a little cart like a hand-barrow, on which were hampers with cabbage and carrots and peas and joints of meat, for the hotel above.

'Wird es viel sein?' asked Alexander of the little gnome. 'Will it be much?'

'Was meint der Herr?' replied the other. 'What does the gentleman say?'

'Der Regen, wir des lang dauern? Will the rain last long?'

'Nein. Nein. Dies ist kein langer Regen.'

So, with his mule, which had to stand exactly at that spot to make droppings, the little man resumed his way, and Hannele and Alexander were the last on the slope. The air smelt steel-cold of rain, and of hot droppings. Alexander watched the rain beat on the shoulders and on the blue skirt of Hannele.

'It is a pity you left your big coat down below,' he said.

'What good is it saying so now!' she replied, pale at the nose with anger.

'Quite,' he said, as his eyes glowed and his brow blackened. 'What good suggesting anything at any time, apparently?'

She turned round on him in the rain, as they stood perched nearly at the summit of that slanting cliff-climb, with a glacier-paw hung almost invisible above, and waters gloating aloud in the gulf below. She faced him, and he faced her.

'What have you ever suggested to me?' she said, her face naked as the rain itself with an ice-bitter fury. 'What have you ever suggested to me?'

'When have you ever been open to suggestion?' he said, his face dark and his eyes curiously glowing.

'I? I? Ha! Haven't I waited for you to suggest something? And all you can do is to come here with a picture to reproach me for having sold your doll. Ha! I'm glad I sold it. A foolish barren effigy it was too, a foolish staring thing. What should I do but sell it. Why should I keep it, do you imagine?'

'Why do you come here with me today, then?'

'Why do I come here with you today?' she replied. 'I come to see the mountains, which are wonderful, and give me strength. And I come to see the glacier. Do you think I come here to see YOU? Why should I? You are always in some hotel or other away below.'

'You came to see the glacier and the mountains WITH me,' he replied.

'Did I? Then I made a mistake. You can do nothing but find fault even with God's mountains.'

A dark flame suddenly went over his face.

'Yes,' he said, 'I hate them, I hate them. I hate their snow and their affectations.'

'AFFECTATION!' she laughed. 'Oh! Even the mountains are affected for you, are they?'

'Yes,' he said. 'Their loftiness and their uplift. I hate their uplift. I hate people prancing on mountain-tops and feeling exalted. I'd like to make them all stop up there, on their mountain-tops, and chew ice to fill their stomachs. I wouldn't let them down again, I wouldn't. I hate it all, I tell you; I hate it.'

She looked in wonder on his dark, glowing, ineffectual face. It seemed to her like a dark flame burning in the daylight and in the ice-rains: very ineffectual and unnecessary.

'You must be a little mad,' she said superbly, 'to talk like that about the mountains. They are so much bigger than you.'

'No,' he said. 'No! They are not.'

'What!' she laughed aloud. 'The mountains are not bigger than you? But you are extraordinary.'

'They are not bigger than me,' he cried. 'Any more than you are bigger than me if you stand on a ladder. They are not bigger than me. They are less than me.'

'Oh! Oh!' she cried in wonder and ridicule.' The mountains are less than you.'

'Yes,' he cried, 'they are less.'

He seemed suddenly to go silent and remote as she watched him. The speech had gone out of his face again, he seemed to be standing a long way off from her, beyond some border-line. And in the midst of her indignant amazement she watched him with wonder and a touch of fascination. To what country did he belong then? — to what dark, different atmosphere?

'You must suffer from megalomania,' she said. And she said what she felt.

But he only looked at her out of dark, dangerous, haughty eyes.

They went on their way in the rain in silence. He was filled with a passionate silence and imperiousness, a curious, dark, masterful force that supplanted thought in him. And she, who always pondered, went pondering: 'Is he mad? What does he mean? Is he a madman? He wants to bully me. He wants to bully me into something. What does he want to bully me into? Does he want me to love him?'

At this final question she rested. She decided that what he wanted was that she should love him. And this thought flattered her vanity and her pride and appeased her wrath against him. She felt quite mollified towards him.

But what a way he went about it! He wanted her to love him. Of this she was sure. He had always wanted her to love him, even from the first. Only he had not made up his MIND about it. He had not made up his mind. After his wife had died he had gone away to make up his mind. Now he had made it up. He wanted her to love him. And he was offended, mortally offended because she had sold his doll.

So, this was the conclusion to which Hannele came. And it pleased her, and it flattered her. And it made her feel quite warm towards him, as they walked in the rain. The rain, by the way, was abating. The spume over the hollow crest to which they were approaching was thinning considerably. They could again see the glacier paw hanging out a little beyond. The rain was going to pass. And they were not far now from the hotel, and the third level of Lammerboden.

He wanted her to love him. She felt again quite glowing and triumphant inside herself, and did not care a bit about the rain on her shoulders. He wanted her to love him. Yes, that was how she had to put it. He didn't want to LOVE her. No. He wanted HER to love HIM.

But then, of course, woman-like, she took his love for granted. So many men had been so very ready to love her. And this one — to her amazement, to her indignation, and rather to her secret satisfaction — just blackly insisted that SHE must love HIM. Very well — she would give him a run for his money. That was it: he blackly insisted that SHE must love HIM. What he felt was not to be considered. SHE must love HIM. And be bullied into it. That was what it amounted to. In his silent, black, overbearing soul, he wanted to compel her, he wanted to have power over her. He wanted to make her love him so that he had power over her. He wanted to bully her, physically, sexually, and from the inside.

And she! Well, she was just as confident that she was not going to be bullied. She would love him: probably she would: most probably she did already. But she was not going to be bullied by him in any way whatsoever. No, he must go down on his knees to her if he wanted her love. And then she would love him. Because she DID love him. But a dark-eyed little master and bully she would never have.

And this was her triumphant conclusion. Meanwhile the rain had almost ceased, they had almost reached the rim of the upper level, towards which they were climbing, and he was walking in that silent diffidence which made her watch him because she was not sure what he was feeling, what he was thinking, or even what he was. He was a puzzle to her: eternally incomprehensible in his feelings and even his sayings. There seemed to her no logic and no reason in what he felt and said. She could never tell what his next mood would come out of. And this made her uneasy, made her watch him. And at the same time it piqued her attention. He had some of the fascination of the incomprehensible. And his curious inscrutable face — it wasn't really only a meaningless mask, because she had seen it half an hour ago melt with a quite incomprehensible and rather, to her mind, foolish passion. Strange, black, inconsequential passion. Asserting with that curious dark ferocity that he was bigger than the mountains. Madness! Madness! Megalomania.

But because he gave himself away, she forgave him and even liked him. And the strange passion of his, that gave out incomprehensible flashes, WAS rather fascinating to her. She felt just a tiny bit sorry for him. But she wasn't going to be bullied by him. She wasn't going to give in to him and his black passion. No, never. It must be love on equal terms or nothing. For love on equal terms she was quite ready. She only waited for him to offer it.

Chapter 17

In the hotel was a buzz of tourists. Alexander and Hannele sat in the restaurant drinking hot coffee and milk, and watching the maidens in cotton frocks and aprons and bare arms, and the fair youths with maidenly necks and huge voracious boots, and the many Jews of the wrong sort and the wrong shape. These Jews were all being very Austrian, in Tyrol costume that didn't sit on them, assuming the whole gesture and intonation of aristocratic Austria, so that you might think they WERE Austrian aristocrats, if you weren't properly listening, or if you didn't look twice. Certainly they were lords of the Alps, or at least lords of the Alpine hotels this summer, let prejudice be what it might. Jews of the wrong sort. And yet even they imparted a wholesome breath of sanity, disillusion, unsentimentality to the excited 'Bergheil' atmosphere. Their dark-eyed, sardonic presence seemed to say to the maidenly-necked mountain youths: 'Don't sprout wings of the spirit too much, my dears.'

The rain had ceased. There was a wisp of sunshine from a grey sky. Alexander left the knapsack, and the two went out into the air. Before them lay the last level of the up-climb, the Lammerboden. It was a rather gruesome hollow between the peaks, a last shallow valley about a mile long. At the end the enormous static stream of the glacier poured in from the blunt mountain-top of ice. The ice was dull, sullen-coloured, melted on the surface by the very hot summer: and so it seemed a huge, arrested, sodden flood, ending in a wave-wall of stone-speckled ice upon the valley bed of rocky débris. A gruesome descent of stone and blocks of rock, the little valley bed, with a river raving through. On the left rose the grey rock, but the glacier was there, sending down great paws of ice. It was like some great, deep-furred ice-bear lying spread upon the top heights, and reaching down terrible paws of ice into the valley: like some immense sky-bear fishing in the earth's solid hollows from above. Hepburn it just filled with terror. Hannele too it scared, but it gave her a sense of ecstasy. Some of the immense, furrowed paws of ice held down between the rock were vivid blue in colour, but of a frightening, poisonous blue, like crystal copper sulphate. Most of the ice was a sullen, semi-translucent greeny grey.

The two set off to walk through the massy, desolate stone-bed, under rocks and over waters, to the main glacier. The flowers were even more beautiful on this last reach. Particularly the dark harebells were large and almost black and ice-metallic: one could imagine they gave a dull ice-chink. And the grass of Parnassus stood erect, white-veined big cups held terribly naked and open to their ice air.

From behind the great blunt summit of ice that blocked the distance at the end of the valley, a pale-grey, woolly mist or cloud was fusing up, exhaling huge, like some grey-dead aura into the sky, and covering the top of the glacier. All the way along the valley people were threading, strangely insignificant, among the grey dishevel of stone and rock, like insects. Hannele and Alexander went ahead quickly, along the tiring track.

'Are you glad now that you came?' she said, looking at him triumphant.

'Very glad I came,' he said. His eyes were dilated with excitement that was ordeal or mystic battle rather than the Bergheil ecstasy. The curious vibration of his excitement made the scene strange, rather horrible to her. She too shuddered. But it still seemed to her to hold the key to all glamour and ecstasy, the great silent, living glacier. It seemed to her like a grand beast.

As they came near they saw the wall of ice: the glacier end, thick crusted and speckled with stone and dirt debris. From underneath, secret in stones, water rushed out. When they came quite near, they saw the great monster was sweating all over, trickles and rivulets of sweat running down his sides of pure, slush-translucent ice. There it was, the glacier, ending abruptly in the wall of ice under which they stood. Near to, the ice was pure, but water-logged, all the surface rather rotten from the hot summer. It was sullenly translucent, and of a watery, darkish bluey-green colour. But near the earth it became again bright coloured, gleams of green like jade, gleams of blue like thin, pale sapphire, in little caverns above the wet stones where the walls trickled for ever.

Alexander wanted to climb on to the glacier. It was his one desire — to stand upon it. So under the pellucid wet wall they toiled among rock upwards, to where the guide-track mounted the ice. Several other people were before them — mere day tourists — and all uncertain about venturing any farther. For the ice-slope rose steep and slithery, pure, sun-locked, sweating ice. Still, it was like a curved back. One could scramble on to it, and on up to the first level, like the flat on top of some huge paw.

There stood the little cluster of people, facing the uphill of sullen, pure, sodden-looking ice. They were all afraid: naturally. But being human, they all wanted to go beyond their fear. It was strange that the ice looked so pure, like flesh. Not bright, because the surface was soft like a soft, deep epidermis. But pure ice away down to immense depths.

Alexander, after some hesitation, began gingerly to try the ice. He was frightened of it. And he had no stick, and only smooth-soled boots. But he had a great desire to stand on the glacier. So, gingerly and shakily, he began to struggle a few steps up the pure slope. The ice was soft on the surface, he could kick his heel in it and get a little sideways grip. So, staggering and going sideways he got up a few yards, and was on the naked ice-slope.

Immediately the youths and the fat man below began to tackle it too: also two maidens. For some time, however, Alexander gingerly and scramblingly led the way. The slope of ice was steeper, and rounded, so that it was difficult to stand up in any way. Sometimes he slipped, and was clinging with burnt finger-ends to the soft ice mass. Then he tried throwing his coat down, and getting a foot-hold on that. Then he went quite quickly by bending down and getting a little grip with his fingers, and going ridiculously as on four legs.

Hannele watched from below, and saw the ridiculous exhibition, and was frightened and amused, but more frightened. And she kept calling, to the great joy of the Austrians down below:

'Come back. Do come back.'

But when he got on to his feet again he only waved his hand at her, half crossly, as she stood away down there in her blue frock. The other fellows with sticks and nail-boots had now taken heart and were scrambling like crabs past our hero, doing better than he.

He had come to a rift in the ice. He sat near the edge and looked down. Clean, pure ice, fused with pale colour, and fused into intense copper-sulphate blue away down in the crack. It was not like crystal, but fused as one fuses a borax bead under a blow-flame. And keenly, wickedly blue in the depths of the crack.

He looked upwards. He had not half mounted the slope. So on he went, upon the huge body of the soft-fleshed ice, slanting his way sometimes on all fours, sometimes using his coat, usually hitting-in with the side of his heel. Hannele down below was crying him to come back. But two other youths were now almost level with him.

So he struggled on till he was more or less over the brim. There he stood and looked at the ice. It came down from above in a great hollow world of ice. A world, a terrible place of hills and valleys and slopes, all motionless, all of ice. Away above the grey mist-cloud was looming bigger. And near at hand were long, huge cracks, side by side, like gills in the ice. It would seem as if the ice breathed through these great ridged gills. One could look down into the series of gulfs, fearful depths, and the colour burning that acid, intense blue, intenser as the crack went deeper. And the crests of the open gills ridged and grouped pale blue above the crevices. It seemed as if the ice breathed there.

The wonder, the terror, and the bitterness of it. Never a warm leaf to unfold, never a gesture of life to give off. A world sufficient unto itself in lifelessness, all this ice.

He turned to go down, though the youths were passing beyond him. And seeing the naked translucent ice heaving downwards in a vicious curve, always the same dark translucency underfoot, he was afraid. If he slipped, he would certainly slither the whole way down, and break some of his bones. Even when he sat down he had to cling with his finger-nails in the ice, because if he had started to slide he would have slid the whole way down on his trouser-seat, precipitously, and have landed heaven knows how.

Hannele was watching from below. And he was frightened, perched, seated on the shoulder of ice and not knowing how to get off. Above he saw the great blue gills of ice ridging the air. Down below were two blue cracks — then the last wet level claws of ice upon the stones. And there stood Hannele and the three or four people who had got so far.

However, he found that by striking in his heels sideways with sufficient sharpness he could keep his footing, no matter how steep the slope. So he started to jerk his way zig-zag downwards.

As he descended, arrived a guide with a black beard and all the paraphernalia of ropes and pole and bristling boots. He and his gentlemen began to strike their way up the ice. With those bristling nails like teeth in one's boots, it was quite easy: and a pole to press on to.

Hannele, who had got sick of waiting, and who was also frightened, had gone scuttling on the return journey. He hurried after her, thankful to be off the ice, but excited and gratified. Looking round, he saw the guide and the men on the ice watching the ice-world and the weather. Then they too turned to come down. The day wasn't safe.

Chapter 18

Pondering, rather thrilled, they threaded their way through the desert of rock and rushing water back to the hotel. The sun was shining warmly for a moment, and he felt happy, though his finger-ends were bleeding a little from the ice.

'But one day,' said Hannele, 'I should love to go with a guide right up, high, right into the glacier.'

'No,' said he. 'I've been far enough. I prefer the world where cabbages will grow on the soil. Nothing grows on glaciers.'

'They say there are glacier fleas, which only live on glaciers,' she said.

'Well, to me the ice didn't look good to eat, even for a flea.'

'You never know,' she laughed. 'But you're glad you've been, aren't you?'

'Very glad. Now I need never go again.'

'But you DID think it wonderful?'

'Marvellous. And awful, to my mind.'

Chapter 19

They ate venison and spinach in the hotel, then set off down again. Both felt happier. She gathered some flowers and put them in her handkerchief so they should not die. And again they sat by the stream, to drink a little wine.

But the fume of cloud was blowing up again, thick from behind the glacier. Hannele was uneasy. She wanted to get down. So they went fairly quickly. Many other tourists were hurrying downwards also. The rain began — a sharp handful of drops flung from beyond the glacier.

So Hannele and he did not stay to rest, but dropped easily down the steep, dark valley towards the motor-car terminus.

There they had tea, rather tired, but comfortably so. The big hotel restaurant was hideous, and seemed sordid. So in the gloom of a grey, early twilight they went out again and sat on a seat, watching the tourists and the trippers and the motor-car men. There were three Jews from Vienna: and the girl had a huge white woolly dog, as big as a calf, and white and woolly and silky and amiable as a toy. The men, of course, came patting it and admiring it, just as men always do, in life and in novels. And the girl, holding the leash, posed and leaned backwards in the attitude of heroines on novel-covers. She said the white cool monster was a Siberian steppe-dog. Alexander wondered what the steppes made of such a wuffer. And the three Jews pretended they were elegant Austrians out of popular romances.

'Do you think,' said Alexander, 'you will marry the Herr Regierungsrat?'

She looked round, making wide eyes.

'It looks like it, doesn't it!' she said.

'Quite,' he said.

Hannele watched the woolly white dog. So of course it came wagging its ever-amiable hindquarters towards her. She looked at it still, but did not touch it.

'What makes you ask such a question?' she said.

'I can't say. But even so, you haven't really answered. Do you really fully intend to marry the Herr Regierungsrat? Is that your final intention at this moment?'

She looked at him again.

'But before I answer,' she said, 'oughtn't I to know why you ask?'

'Probably you know already,' he said.

'I assure you I don't.'

He was silent for some moments. The huge, woolly dog stood in front of him and breathed enticingly, with its tongue out. He only looked at it blankly.

'Well,' he said, 'if you were not going to marry the Herr Regierungsrat, I should suggest that you marry me.'

She stared away at the auto-garage, a very faint look of amusement, or pleasure, or ridicule on her face: or all three. And a certain shyness.

'But why?' she said.

'Why what?' he returned.

'Why should you suggest that I should marry you?'

'WHY?' he replied, in his lingering tones. 'WHY? Well, for what purpose does a man usually ask a woman to marry him?'

'For what PURPOSE!' she repeated, rather haughtily.

'For what reason, then!' he corrected.

She was silent for some moments. Her face was closed and a little numb-looking, her hands lay very still in her lap. She looked away from him, across the road.

'There is usually only one reason,' she replied, in a rather small voice.

'Yes?' he replied curiously. 'What would you say that was?'

She hesitated. Then she said, rather stiffly:

'Because he really loved her, I suppose. That seems to me the only excuse for a man asking a woman to marry him.'

Followed a dead silence, which she did not intend to break. He knew he would have to answer, and for some reason he didn't want to say what was obviously the thing to say.

'Leaving aside the question of whether you love me or I love you — ' he began.

'I certainly WON'T leave it aside,' she said.

'And I certainly won't consider it,' he said, just as obstinately.

She turned now and looked full at him, with amazement, ridicule, and anger in her face.

'I really think you must be mad,' she said.

'I doubt if you do think that,' he replied. 'It is only a method of retaliation, that is. I think you understand my point very clearly.'

'Your point!' she cried. 'Your point! Oh, so you have a point in all this palavering?'

'Quite!' said he.

She was silent with indignation for some time. Then she said angrily:

'I assure you I do NOT see your point. I don't see any point at all. I see only impertinence.'

'Very good,' he replied. 'The point is whether we marry on a basis of love.'

'Indeed! Marry! We, marry! I don't think that is by any means the point.'

He took his knapsack from under the seat between his feet. And from the knapsack he took the famous picture.

'When,' he said, 'we were supposed to be in love with one another, you made that doll of me, didn't you?' And he sat looking at the odious picture.

'I never for one moment deluded myself that you REALLY loved me,' she said bitterly.

'Take the other point, whether YOU loved ME or not,' said he.

'How could I love you when I couldn't believe in your love for me?' she cried.

He put the picture down between his knees again.

'All this about love,' he said, 'is very confusing and very complicated.'

'Very! In YOUR case. Love to me is simple enough,' she said.

'Is it? Is it? And was it simple love which made you make that doll of me?'

'Why shouldn't I make a doll of you? Does it do you any harm? And WEREN'T you a doll, good heavens! You WERE nothing but a doll. So what hurt does it do you?'

'Yes, it does. It does me the greatest possible damage,' he replied.

She turned on him with wide-open eyes of amazement and rage.

'Why? Pray why? Can you tell me why?'

'Not quite, I can't,' he replied, taking up the picture and holding it in front of him. She turned her face from it as a cat turns its nose away from a lighted cigarette.' But when I look at it — when I look at this — then I KNOW that there is no love between you and me.'

'Then why are you talking at me in this shameful way?' she flashed at him, tears of anger and mortification rising to her eyes. 'You want your little revenge on me, I suppose, because I made that doll of you.'

'That may be so, in a small measure,' he said.

'That is ALL. That is all and everything,' she cried. 'And that is all you came back to me for — for this petty revenge. Well, you've had it now. But please don't speak to me any more. I shall see if I can go home in the big omnibus.'

She rose and walked away. He saw her hunting for the motor-bus conductor. He saw her penetrate into the yard of the garage. And he saw her emerge again, after a time, and take the path to the river. He sat on in front of the hotel. There was nothing else to do.

The tourists who had arrived in the big bus now began to collect. And soon the huge, drab vehicle itself rolled up and stood big as a house before the hotel door. The passengers began to scramble into their seats. The two men of the white dog were going: but the woman of the white dog, and the dog, were staying behind. Hepburn wondered if Hannele had managed to get herself transferred. He doubted it, because he knew the omnibus was crowded.

Moreover, he had her ticket.

The passengers were packed in. The conductor was collecting the tickets. And at last the great bus rolled away. The bay of the road-end seemed very empty. Even the woman with the white dog had gone. Soon the other car, the Luxus, so-called, must appear. Hepburn sat and waited. The evening was falling chilly, the trees looked gruesome.

At last Hannele sauntered up again, unwillingly.

'I think,' she said, 'you have my ticket.'

'Yes, I have,' he replied.

'Will you give it me, please?'

He gave it to her. She lingered a moment. Then she walked away.

There was the sound of a motor-car. With a triumphant purr the Luxus came steering out of the garage yard and drew up at the hotel door. Hannele came hastening also. She went straight to one of the hinder doors — she and Hepburn had their seats in front, beside the driver. She had her foot on the step of the back seat. And then she was afraid. The little sharp-faced driver — there was no conductor — came round looking at the car. He looked at her with his sharp, metallic eye of a mechanic.

'Are all the people going back who came?' she asked, shrinking.

'Jawohl.'

'It is full — this car?'

'Jawohl.'

'There's no other place?'

'Nein.'

Hannele shrank away. The driver was absolutely laconic.

Six of the passengers were here: four were already seated. Hepburn sat still by the hotel door, Hannele lingered in the road by the car, and the little driver, with a huge woollen muffler round his throat, was running round and in and out looking for the two missing passengers. Of course there were two missing passengers. No, he could not find them. And off he trotted again, silently, like a weasel after two rabbits. And at last, when everybody was getting cross, he unearthed them and brought them scuttling to the car.

Now Hannele took her seat, and Hepburn beside her. The driver snapped up the tickets and climbed in past them. With a vindictive screech the car glided away down the ravine. Another beastly trip was over, another infernal joyful holiday done with.

'I think,' said Hepburn, 'I may as well finish what I had to say.'

'What?' cried Hannele, fluttering in the wind of the rushing car.

'I may as well finish what I had to say,' shouted he, his breath blown away.

'Finish then,' she screamed, the ends of her scarf flickering behind her.

'When my wife died,' he said loudly, 'I knew I couldn't love any more.'

'Oh — h!' she screamed ironically.

'In fact,' he shouted, 'I realized that, as far as I was concerned, love was a mistake.'

'WHAT was a mistake?' she screamed.

'Love,' he bawled.

'Love!' she screamed. 'A mistake?' Her tone was derisive.

'For me personally,' he said, shouting.

'Oh, only for you personally,' she cried, with a pouf of laughter.

The car gave a great swerve, and she fell on the driver. Then she righted herself. It gave another swerve, and she fell on Alexander. She righted herself angrily. And now they ran straight on: and it seemed a little quieter.

'I realized,' he said, 'that I had always made a mistake, undertaking to love.'

'It must have been an undertaking for you,' she cried.

'Yes, I'm afraid it was. I never really wanted it. But I thought I did. And that's where I made my mistake.'

'Whom have you ever loved? — even as an undertaking?' she asked.

'To begin with, my mother: and that was a mistake. Then my sister: and that was a mistake. Then a girl I had known all my life: and that was a mistake. Then my wife: and that was my most terrible mistake. And then I began the mistake of loving you.'

'Undertaking to love me, you mean,' she said. 'But then you never did properly undertake it. You never really UNDERTOOK to love me.'

'Not quite, did I?' said he.

And she sat feeling angry that he had never made the undertaking.

'No,' he continued. 'Not quite. That is why I came back to you. I don't want to love you. I don't want marriage on a basis of love.'

'On a basis of what, then?'

'I think you know without my putting it into words,' he said.

'Indeed, I assure you I don't. You are much too mysterious,' she replied.

Talking in a swiftly-running motor-car is a nerve-racking business. They both had a pause, to rest, and to wait for a quieter stretch of road.

'It isn't very easy to put it into words,' he said. 'But I tried marriage once on a basis of love, and I must say it was a ghastly affair in the long run. And I believe it would be so, for me, WHATEVER woman I had.'

'There must be something wrong with you, then,' said she.

'As far as love goes. And yet I want marriage. I want marriage. I want a woman to honour and obey me.'

'If you are quite reasonable and VERY sparing with your commands,' said Hannele. 'And very careful how you give your orders.'

'In fact, I want a sort of patient Griselda. I want to be honoured and obeyed. I don't want love.'

'How Griselda managed to honour that fool of a husband of hers, even if she obeyed him, is more than I can say,' said Hannele. 'I'd like to know what she REALLY thought of him. Just what any woman thinks of a bullying fool of a husband.'

'Well,' said he, 'that's no good to me.'

They were silent now until the car stopped at the station. There they descended and walked on under the trees by the lake.

'Sit on a seat,' he said, 'and let us finish.'

Hannele, who was really anxious to hear what he should say, and who, woman-like, was fascinated by a man when he began to give away his own inmost thoughts — no matter how much she might jeer afterwards — sat down by his side. It was a grey evening, just falling dark. Lights twinkled across the lake, the hotel over there threaded its strings of light. Some little boats came rowing quietly to shore. It was a grey, heavy evening, with that special sense of dreariness with which a public holiday usually winds up.

'Honour and obedience: and the proper physical feelings,' he said. 'To me that is marriage. Nothing else.'

'But what are the proper physical feelings but love?' asked Hannele.

'No,' he said. 'A woman wants you to adore her, and be in love with her — and I shan't. I will not do it again, if I live a monk for the rest of my days. I will neither adore you nor be in love with you.'

'You won't get a chance, thank you. And what do you call the proper physical feelings, if you are not in love? I think you want something vile.'

'If a woman honours me — absolutely from the bottom of her nature honours me — and obeys me because of that, I take it, my desire for her goes very much deeper than if I was in love with her, or if I adored her.'

'It's the same thing. If you love, then everything is there — all the lot: your honour and obedience and everything. And if love isn't there, nothing is there,' she said.

'That isn't true,' he replied. 'A woman may love you, she may adore you, but she'll never honour you nor obey you. The most loving and adoring woman today could any minute start and make a doll of her husband — as you made of me.'

'Oh, that eternal doll. What makes it stick so in your mind?'

'I don't know. But there it is. It wasn't malicious. It was flattering, if you like. But it just sticks in me like a thorn: like a thorn. And there it is, in the world, in Germany somewhere. And you can say what you like, but ANY woman, today, no matter HOW much she loves her man — she could start any minute and make a doll of him. And the doll would be her hero: and her hero would be no more than her doll. My wife might have done it. She did do it, in her mind. She had her doll of me right enough. Why, I heard her talk about me to other women. And her doll was a great deal sillier than the one you made. But it's all the same. If a woman loves you, she'll make a doll out of you. She'll never be satisfied till she's made your doll. And when she's got your doll, that's all she wants. And that's what love means. And so, I won't be loved. And I won't love. I won't have anybody loving me. It is an insult. I feel I've been insulted for forty years: by love, and the women who've loved me. I won't be loved. And I won't love. I'll be honoured and I'll be obeyed: or nothing.'

'Then it'll most probably be nothing,' said Hannele sarcastically. 'For I assure you I've nothing but love to offer.'

'Then keep your love,' said he.

She laughed shortly.

'And you?' she cried. 'You! Even suppose you WERE honoured and obeyed. I suppose all you've got to do is to sit there like a sultan and sup it up.'

'Oh no. I have many things to do. And woman or no woman, I'm going to start to do them.'

'What, pray?'

'Why, nothing very exciting. I'm going to East Africa to join a man who's breaking his neck to get his three thousand acres of land under control. And when I've done a few more experiments and observations, and got all the necessary facts, I'm going to do a book on the moon. Woman or no woman, I'm going to do that.'

'And the woman? — supposing you get the poor thing.'

'Why, she'll come along with me, and we'll set ourselves up out there.'

'And she'll do all the honouring and obeying and housekeeping incidentally, while you ride about in the day and stare at the moon in the night.'

He did not answer. He was staring away across the lake.

'What will you do for the woman, poor thing, while she's racking herself to pieces honouring you and obeying you and doing frightful housekeeping in Africa: because I know it can be AWFUL: awful.'

'Well,' he said slowly, 'she'll be my wife, and I shall treat her as such. If the marriage service says love and cherish — well, in that sense I shall do so.'

'Oh!' cried Hannele. 'What, LOVE her? Actually love the poor thing?'

'Not in that sense of the word, no. I shan't adore her or be in love with her. But she'll be my wife, and I shall love and cherish her as such.'

'Just because she's your wife. Not because she's herself. Ghastly fate for any miserable woman,' said Hannele.

'I don't think so. I think it's her highest fate.'

'To be your wife?'

'To be a wife — and to be loved and shielded as a wife — not as a flirting woman.'

'To be loved and cherished just because you're his wife! No, thank you. All I can admire is the conceit and impudence of it.'

'Very well, then — there it is,' he said, rising.

She rose too, and they went on towards where the boat was tied.

As they were rowing in silence over the lake, he said:

'I shall leave tomorrow.'

She made no answer. She sat and watched the lights of the villa draw near. And then she said:

'I'll come to Africa with you. But I won't promise to honour and obey you.'

'I don't want you otherwise,' he said, very quietly.

The boat was drifting to the little landing-stage. Hannele's friends were hallooing to her from the balcony.

'Hallo!' she cried. 'Ja. Da bin ich. Ja, 's war wunderschön.'

Then to him she said:

'You'll come in?'

'No,' he said, 'I'll row straight back.'

From the villa they were running down the steps to meet Hannele.

'But won't you have me even if I love you?' she asked him.

'You must promise the other,' he said. 'It comes in the marriage service.'

'Hat 's geregnet? Wiewar das Wetter? Warst du auf dem Gletscher?' cried the voices from the garden.

'Nein — kein Regen. Wunderschön! Ja, er war ganz auf dem Gletscher,' cried Hannele in reply. And to him, sotto voce:

'Don't be a solemn ass. Do come in.'

'No,' he said, 'I don't want to come in.'

'Do you want to go away tomorrow? Go if you DO. But, anyway, I won't say it BEFORE the marriage service. I needn't, need I?'

She stepped from the boat on to the plank.

'Oh,' she said, turning round, 'give me that picture, please, will you? I want to burn it.'

He handed it to her.
'And come tomorrow, will you?' she said.
'Yes, in the morning.'
He pulled back quickly into the darkness.

www.ingramcontent.com/pod-product-compliance
Lightning Source LLC
LaVergne TN
LVHW051016080826
845145LV00009B/2657

* 9 7 8 1 6 4 4 3 9 0 3 4 4 *